THE SURVIVOR

AND OTHER TALES OF OLD SAN FRANCISCO

STEVE BARTHOLOMEW

DARK GOPHER BOOKS

Author's note: These stories were originally published, one at a time, by Amazon Direct as ebook only.

Cover art is courtesy of Francis Samuel Marryat, published under creative commons license.

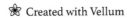 Created with Vellum

1

THE SURVIVOR

SAN FRANCISCO, 1847

The survivor showed up one morning in Hyram Courtenay's front yard. He didn't come up and knock on the front door, he just stood there by the yard gate, waiting. Hyram had stepped out on his way to the warehouse. He blinked a couple of times, looking at the silent figure, wondering if the fellow meant harm. At first glance he thought him an older man, but then realized by his unlined face he could not be more than sixteen. The boy looked back and didn't move.

Hyram filled his pipe with shag cut, struck a match and sucked in some smoke, watching the fellow out of half shut eyes. Then he advanced across the yard. "Need somethin'?"

The boy looked at him. Up close, Hyram could tell he was scrawny, as if he'd been missing a few meals. The boy said, "Somebody told me I might find work."

Hyram tried a smile but the boy looked deadly serious, as if he'd forgotten how to grin.

"It's true I might could use a little help. What's your name, mister?"

"I ain't no mister. Name's Lucas." He hesitated, licked his lips. "Lucas Cavanaugh."

Hyram got the feeling that wasn't a real name. But then it didn't matter to him. A fellow might change his name for any number of reasons. If he was wanted for murder or bank robbery that wasn't Hyram's business. "How long you been here? In this town, I mean?"

Lucas looked around, as if to make sure he knew which town Hyram referred to. "San Francisco? Only a couple weeks, sir. When I started out back east I thought I was headed for Yerba Buena. Then I come to find out they just changed the name."

"That they did. Come along and we'll talk." He placed an arm around the boy's shoulder and started out the gate. "This city's getting bigger and busier. They tell me there's about eight hundred fifty souls here altogether now, and growing all the time. A few years ago there weren't but four or five houses. Now look. There's lots of work, if that's what you're after. Did you come here with family?"

"No sir." Lucas hesitated, then added, "That is, I did but they died. Ma and pa, I mean."

Hyram looked sharply at him, but decided not to ask how. Instead, after a moment he said, "You must have heard I have a warehouse, down by the docks at Mission Bay. I stock mainly rawhide and tallow. I ship all over, to China, the Sandwich Islands and east to the States. I have a couple Indians working for me now, but it's true I could use another hand, if you don't mind hard work. I can let you have a dollar a day."

"That would be fine, sir. I can start right now."

Hyram looked him up and down. The boy wore canvas trousers and a wool shirt. They were clean but a bit ragged. "Did you have breakfast, Mister Cavanaugh? It doesn't do to work on an empty stomach."

Lucas shook his head without looking at Hyram. Hyram pressed a silver quarter into his palm. "An advance on your first day. You pop into that chop house over there and get yourself a stack of waffles. When you're done come on down to my warehouse. Anybody will point it out to you."

Later that morning the boy showed up. It had crossed Hyram's mind that perhaps he had merely meant to cadge a quarter and move on. Instead he looked ready to work. But Hyram didn't like the way his eyes kept shifting right and left, as if he expected attack.

Yesterday a ship had anchored in the harbor, awaiting a change of cargo. Some of the trade goods, mostly men's and lady's clothes, landed in Hyram's warehouse, to be exchanged for stacks of rawhide and barrels of tallow. Hyram showed Lucas what he wanted moved on the hand truck, and the boy went to work quickly, asking few questions.

"They're planning to build us a pier soon," Hyram said. "In the meantime, men have to row goods across to the ship. That can be hard going when it rains."

Only one of Hyram's Indians, Luis, had shown up for work that day. Hyram asked him about the other man, Carlos. "Sick," Luis said. Hyram shrugged. Maybe Carlos would return tomorrow, maybe not. Watching Lucas wrestle a barrel onto the truck, he said, "Luis could help you with that if you want."

Lucas shook his head. "That's all right sir."

Hyram had noticed how he kept glancing in Luis's direction. "Didn't you ever see an Indian before?"

"Yes sir, on the trip west."

Hyram checked off another barrel on his ledger. "You needn't worry, he's Miwok, not Comanche. He won't scalp you. He's a good Catholic. Aren't you, Luis?" The Indian nodded, went on with his labor.

The work day ended after sunset. Hyram locked the warehouse door and handed Lucas some coins. "Here's the balance for your day's work. I'm paying you in Mexico silver. Don't worry, it's good currency here. We don't see too many dollars yet. Maybe someday we'll have our own mint. Till then we make do. Get back here at eight tomorrow morning if you want more work."

" Yes sir. Thank you, sir."

The boy started to turn away, but Hyram touched his shoulder. Lucas jumped, then turned back. "Sir?"

"Where you been staying, lad?"

Lucas shrugged. "There's a fellow lets me sleep in his horse barn if I keep it swept up. It's warm enough, I guess."

"Won't be warm in a month or so, when the rains come. Why don't you come and have dinner tonight with me and the missus? Maybe we can work something out. Ain't nothing worse than sleeping in the cold."

At that, Lucas's eyes widened. "No sir. Ain't nothing worse!"

They walked back to Hyram's home mainly in silence; they were both tired. Hyram looked forward to an after-dinner smoke. Lisbeth usually cooked more than the both of them could eat, so he had no worries about not warning her of an extra mouth.

When they walked in, she looked a bit startled, but then gave a huge smile and took both of Lucas's hands. "How nice to have a guest for a change! And such a fair looking lad! Now, you both go get washed up while I set an extra table!"

"Did the water wagon come?" Hyram asked.

"Of course. There's plenty of water in the tank. Now, both of you wash behind your ears!"

At the wash basin in the back room, Hyram patted his own stomach. "Looks like you might could use some of Lisbeth's cooking. But a little too often, you're like to get a belly like mine."

Lucas finished washing his face and hands and began drying with an old flour sack. Suddenly he looked Hyram in the eye and blurted, "I can't eat meat, sir."

Hyram blinked, a bit surprised. "Oh? Well. I guess you're one of them vegetarians, then. I've heard of that, never met one. But that's just fine, you can have double of everything else."

Lisbeth served a well-cooked pot roast, with potatoes, carrots and fresh-baked bread. She made no comment when Hyram told her the boy wanted no meat, merely nodded. Lucas put away a full plate of vegetables; when offered seconds he nodded. "Yes ma'am, if you please." Half way through that plate, with both of them watching, he paused and looked up. "I'm not one of them, what you call it, vegetarians. Just can't eat meat, anymore. I do apologize."

"Now, no need for that. It's all the more for the rest of us. You can sleep in our store room tonight. We'll make up a bed for you. Later maybe we can work out something better."

"Yes sir. I do thank you, sir."

Lisbeth gave Hyram a quizzical expression. They had been together long enough to read each other's minds. Hyram knew this expression meant, Do you know what you're doing? Hyram grinned back, which meant *I think I do.*

Lisbeth served apple cobbler for dessert, which Lucas practically inhaled. After supper he offered to help with the dishes, but Lisbeth turned him down, telling him to save his energy for the warehouse. Hyram smoked his pipe; Lucas sat awkwardly watching, his eyes heavy. "Do you like to read, son? Books are hard to come by here, but we do have a few. Also some back issues of the papers."

"Thank you, sir, but I confess I'm some tired. I guess I'll turn in."

Hyram made up bedding on the floor of the store room; Lucas lay down and was snoring before Hyram left. Later, in bed, Lisbeth said, "That boy doesn't talk much."

"No, he don't. I mean doesn't. I get the feeling he's been through a lot. I guess he'll talk when he wants to. I think maybe his parents were killed by Indians."

In the dark of night, Hyram awoke to the sound of the boy talking in his sleep. Several times he moaned.

Next day, there were no new ships in the bay, so work was light. Some goods had to be moved as they were bought or sold. Other than that, chores consisted mainly of inventory, cleaning up, and the constant war against rats and other critters. Hyram could have laid off one or two of his men, but he preferred keeping them on the payroll so they would be there when needed. On Friday a China clipper arrived with a cargo of silks, porcelain and opium, so there was plenty of work. The warehouse began to strain at its adobe walls.

Through it all, Hyram kept an eye on Lucas. He noticed the boy never smiled, not even when someone cracked a joke. It was as if Lucas had no sense of humor. Sometimes, when not busy, he would sit and stare into space. On Sunday Hyram asked him if he might like to attend church. Lucas nodded in agreement, without showing any enthusiasm. He had retrieved an old trunk from the horse barn where he had been staying. From it he produced a threadbare suit, with shirt and tie. They hung loosely on his frame, but he did look more respectable. Hyram nodded at the trunk. "You brought that from the east, I guess?"

"Yes sir. From Illinois." That was as much information about his origin as he had ever ventured, but Hyram did not pursue.

"We don't have a regular church," Hyram said. "But we use the school house on Sunday. The Catholics and Protestants take turns." Lucas nodded without revealing any preference. Hyram and Lisbeth were Protestant, so that was where they went. At the services people turned their heads in curiosity at this stranger in town. Hyram introduced him to a few friends as his new hired man. Without exception they glanced at the boy's face, shook his hand, and then turned away without attempting conversation.

On Monday Lisbeth found a neighbor willing to rent a spare room for fifty cents a week if Lucas would agree to keep the yard cleaned up. He moved his trunk into the new room.

Lucas kept showing up for work and working hard. Over the next month or so, he seemed to gain a little weight. Several times he came to Hyram and Lisbeth's for supper. He also attended church and purchased a new coat from his pay. Hyram thought the boy had no vices, at least not that he could see. When Lisbeth fixed his supper there was no meat on the table, though he did sometimes eat eggs or cheese. Hyram met the neighbor who was renting Lucas his room. He learned nothing, except that the boy was quiet and spent most of his free time reading or working in the vegetable garden.

Probably Hyram never would have learned the truth, had it not been for the robbers. On a Saturday evening after a long day of work, Hyram had invited Lucas for supper and services the next day. A little past sunset, they were walking home and took a shortcut behind one of the city's several gambling houses. Suddenly two men appeared from the darkness, one on each side.

"We'll have your wallets now," one of them demanded. A large knife in his hand glinted in moonlight. Hyram stopped, raised his hands.

"Gentlemen, please —"

"No you won't," Lucas said. He took a step forward, then spun about so he was facing both men. He took something from inside his coat. After a moment Hyram realized it was a hammer, probably from his warehouse.

"You will have nothing," Lucas said. "Except death." His voice sounded not just mature, but old, *ancient.*

Hyram tried to speak, "Son, don't—"

The man with the knife darted forward, stabbing. Lucas was quicker, swung the hammer at the man's wrist. The man screamed and dropped the knife. Now the other man moved, pointing something. Hyram could see it was an old pepperbox pistol.

"You wanna*die?*"

Lucas turned to face him. He spoke in a cold voice. "I already died, sir. I have nought to lose. But you still have your life. If you wish to keep it, *go.* I am Death."

The man tried to cock his pistol, but his hand shook. He nearly dropped it. Lucas stood not moving, waiting. Hyram held his breath without knowing. Finally the man with the broken wrist with his good hand grabbed his friend's shoulder. "He's crazy, Charlie. Let's go." After a moment the pistol disappeared, the two backed off and vanished through the back door of the gambling hall.

Lucas stood immobile, watching them leave. Hyram approached, took the hammer from his hand. He put one arm about the boy's shoulder. Lucas was trembling. Up close, he could see tears on the boy's face. Hyram shoved a bandanna into his hand and watched him blow his nose.

"Come with me." Hyram got him moving. They turned a corner and walked one block to the nearest ale house. Inside, they took a corner table. The place was noisy with Saturday night arguments, speeches and gaming, but not quite rowdy. Although Hyram rarely drank spirits, he got a bottle and poured two glasses, pushing one into the boy's hand. After a moment Lucas drank almost automatically, then went into a coughing fit.

When he was quiet once more, Hyram said, "Last year the Committee of Vigilance chased most of the bad crowd out of town, but we still don't have a regular constabulary. We're hoping the new alcalde will get one organized. That was a brave thing you did back there, but a foolish one. You might have been killed." Lucas said nothing, merely stared at his glass.

Hyram recalled what the boy had said to the robbers. *I already died.* Then at last he remembered reading the story in the *California Star,* a few months back. The paper had called it Starved Camp. For some reason he had failed to make the connection. Perhaps his mind had simply refused to do so. Suddenly his eyes widened in horrid surmise. Quickly he swallowed his whisky.

"You said you had only been in town a few days, when we first met, son. Where were you before that?"

Lucas looked at nothing in particular. "Sutter's Fort for awhile, sir. I don't recollect exactly how long."

"And before that?"

Lucas shrugged. Hyram already knew the answer. The time frame was right. He had come over by wagon train, last winter. Hyram had read the detailed accounts in the paper. He could not imagine going through such horror and remaining sane. And yet, though knowing, he felt forced to ask.

"What was the name of your party, son?"

Lucas stared at things Hyram hoped never himself to see.

"It was Donner," Lucas whispered. "The Donner Party."

2

HEZZIE

I am Hyram Courtenay. Since Lisbeth and I arrived in San Francisco we have almost got used to seeing weird and strange things. We moved here from the east because this was a quiet Mexican pueblo called Yerba Buena, a place where we could live in peace and maybe make a decent living. Then they changed the name, and someone had to go and find gold. Hasn't been any peace since.

Not that I'm complaining, it's just that sometimes events move too quickly for an older couple like ourselves to understand. Like what happened to Hezzie. I got the story from her not once, but several times because I had a hard time believing it. Besides I wanted to be sure I had all the details before writing it down.

Hezzie lived by herself in a cabin up on Rincon Hill, which at the time wasn't much populated. Nobody knew when she arrived or how she got there or why; she just showed up one day and went into business. Her business was fixing people, I mean sick or injured folks. She never said she was a doctor, but she knew about herbs and such. She called herself a midwife, but back then there weren't that many women in the city likely to have babies. We did have the other kind of women, the ones that worked for a living if you catch my drift. Hezzie could patch up gunshot wounds and fix broken bones and tend to grippe and fever, and those skills were sorely needed. When not doing business she pretty much kept to herself, and most folks let her be. If you didn't know, Hezzie is short for Hezekiah. I never did find out her last name.

In those early days San Francisco had a lot of crime, specially before the second Committee of Vigilance got organized. We had our share of duels and bar room brawls and grudge fights. We were also bothered by more organized crime, such as the Sidney Coves, that some called the Sidney Ducks. Now Sheriff Hays has started getting matters under control, but two or three years ago the town was still wild. Even more than now.

As Hezzie tells it, she was pulling up weeds in her vegetable garden when the two strangers showed up. They both looked dirty, as if they'd been sleeping outside for a few days. One of them wore a Colt revolver, the other wore a big bandage wrapped around his arm.

"You Miss Hezekiah?" the one with the gun said. She nodded, looking them over and not much liking what she saw. "I am she. Who's asking?"

"My partner here was in a little scrape last night at a saloon. Just a misunderstanding. I'm told you could patch him up."

Hezzie put down her hoe. "Come on inside."

They went into her house. It was only one room. But it was an old adobe from before the Gold Rush, so it was a better house than many that have gone up since. The men still hadn't given their names. She had the wounded sit backwards in a chair, the better to look at his shoulder. His shirt was soaked with blood, so she had to cut it off with scissors. She looked at the other man. "I'll need some hot water. Do you mind filling that basin from the tank in back? I'll fire up the stove."

Pretty soon she had the wound cleaned up. As she worked the man in the chair kept squeezing his jaw and making groaning noises. She said, "That's a nasty cut. Looks like it was made by a dull knife. I need to sew it up." Though it was a warm day the gunman was sitting by the stove,. He shrugged. "You go right ahead." So far the wounded man hadn't said a word.

Hezzie got out her sewing box and found some white silk thread and went to work. When she was finished her patient, pale and sweating, looked about to faint. She tied on a clean bandage and put his arm in a sling. "You can have a drop of brandy now. I've a bottle there on the shelf." The gunman got up and found the bottle. He inspected the label and gave a low whistle.

"Pretty nice booze for this town. We usually only see rotgut whisky."

She took the bottle from his hand and poured a small draft to hand it to the patient. "It was a gift from one of my customers. You can take those stitches out in a couple of weeks. If you should like to pay me now, that will be one dollar gold or silver."

The man with the gun turned and sat down again and folded his arms. "Do you know who I am, Miss Hezekiah?"

She looked at him. "Can't say I've had the pleasure."

"The name is Johnny Burns. My friend here is Bill Hooks. We're both from Australia."

"I recognized the accent."

"We're both Sidney Coves. We're wanted by the Law."

Hezzie continued watching him in silence.

"In fact," Burns went on, "I'm known in common parlance as "Rackety Jack. My professional name, you might say. There's a bounty of five hundred dollars on my head. Bill here doesn't yet have a price on him."

"You do tell."

Bill licked his lips and narrowed his eyes. Hezzie thought he might be wondering why she had not yet shown fear of him. Johnny Burns went on, "The fact is, Miss Hezekiah, there's a group of citizens what are hot on our heels, as they say. It was one of them what inflicted that ugly wound on my friend Bill, here. So therefore it might seem a good idea that we depart this fair city for awhile, till things cool off. What do you think? Well, anyway Bill here is in agreement." He fell silent, watching her.

After a moment or two she said, "What is your point, sir?"

He shrugged. "Only that I'm afraid we must impose upon your

hospitality. We plan to spend the night here in your fair home. In the morning early we shall be on our way, and you will have our thanks."

"And do I have something to say in this decision?"

He laughed and shook his head. "Now, if you don't mind, Miss, we're both pretty hungry, Bill and me. We're missing a couple of meals or three. What sorta tuck would you have?"

"Tuck?"

"Food. What have you to eat?"

She glanced around the room. One entire wall was lined with shelves full of small bottles, vials and cans, her medicine and herb stock. Near the stove was a cupboard where she kept food. "Look for yourself. I have potatoes and cabbage. I don't know how long you have been in this city, but you may know there's a shortage of food. We used to get a fair amount from across the bay, but a lot of the farmers have gone off to the mines. What with all the new people, the food we have is costly and scarce. I'm not a rich person. Cabbage and potatoes is all I can offer you."

"Speaking of rich, where do you keep your money?"

She stared at him for a moment. Burns grinned and shrugged, waiting. She knew she would have to answer. "The box beneath the bed."

Burns reached under and took out a small wooden box with a lid. "That's all?" She stared back at him. He shrugged again, pocketing the few coins.

"I'll put the food on," she said. She got the cabbage from her cupboard and put a pot on the stove to boil. He watched her find a knife and begin chopping. His hand was near his gun butt. As she was putting in the peeled potatoes with some salt and pepper he suddenly got to his feet and said, "I don't believe you."

"Sir?" She paused in her stirring. She glanced behind him to see that Bill was slumped in a corner, asleep.

"I don't believe that's all you have. Either food or money. When I was sitting near the stove I got a whiff of meat."

She shook her head without looking at him. He came closer and grabbed her upper arm, giving her a shake. "Please, sir, you do harm."

"I'll do more than harm if you try to hold back or cross me. I want that meat for dinner. We'll look for the cash later."

"Please, Mister Burns. That bit of meat is for a poor woman who expects a baby. She has little enough, and requires meat for her child."

"That's too bad. Me and Bill here also requires meat. We have a hard road ahead of us. You been holding back on us. Now, where do you have that cache?" He advanced on her, raising a fist.

"Sir, please don't strike me. It's in that cooler box over in the corner. That's all I have."

Burns found the box. It was behind a small door on the north wall; the box hung outside the house, cooled by breezes. He reached inside and brought out a small object wrapped in linen.

"Here, you take it. I see it's ham, though it ain't much. You cook it, Bill and me eat it." He plopped it down next to the stove. Hezzie removed the wrapping, cut off several large chunks of ham and dropped them in the pot.

"I'm sorry I don't have onions. It would be better with onions."

Burns laughed. "It be better with caviar and champagne. You'll be sorrier if it ain't cooked right. You throw the rest of that meat in the pot."

"It's mostly bone. Surely you don't plan to eat it all?"

He found a plug of tobacco from somewhere in his vest, bit off a chew and spat on the floor. "Bill and me got a long row to hoe."

The pot boiled, Hezzie stirred. In due course she announced it was done. The man who called himself Rackety Jack shook Bill by his bad shoulder. Bill awoke with a curse, "*Damn*, Jack!"

"Time to eat. Get yourself to the table."

Hezzie served them both in tin bowls. She started to serve a third, but Burns clamped a hand on her wrist. "Nothing doing. This tuck is for me and Bill, there ain't enough for three."

Hezzie backed off. "Nothing for poor Hezzie, sir? You are a cruel man." Burns laughed.

Bill put some ham in his mouth and began to chew. "Tastes funny."

Burns shrugged. "Don't care for Miss Hezekiah's cookin'? Don't worry, Bill. It ain't poisoned. I was watchin' all the time, she didn't have time to add poison." He looked at Hezzie and winked. "You didn't add no poison, did you dear?" She merely looked back at him. He laughed again.

The two of them ate all the ham and most of the cabbage and potatoes. When they were done, Bill said, "Are we going to leave her alive?"

Burns gave a broad grin. "Now, why would we want to hurt old Hezekiah, here? By the time she gets over to the sheriff's office we'll be long gone." He winked at Hezzie. "Don't you worry, m'dear. We'll not harm a hair on your grey head." Hezzie knew of course they were lying. She was alive now only because they had needed a cook. She took a chair near the stove and lighted a lantern. By now it was after sunset. She picked up a piece of needlework and began to sew.

"What's the plan?" Bill asked.

Burns spat tobacco juice on the floor. He tossed Bill a thin cigar. "I figure we'll head on down to Mission San Jose. I know a couple places we can hole up there. Maybe in a month or so we can come back and take up where we left off."

Bill shook his head. "I dunno, Jack. I hear the Committee is pretty eager to have a chat with you." He meant the Committee of Vigilance. It was they who had posted the reward on Jack's head. Jack leaned back against the wall and admired the ceiling. "Well, there's always Mexico. Now, listen Bill. You already had some shut eye, so it's my turn. We shall take turns standing watch. You stay awake while I get me some sleep. Wake me up in four hours, hear?"

Bill didn't look happy, but he nodded. "What about her?"

"Just keep your eye peeled. If she tries anything funny let me know." He rolled into Hezzie's bed without removing his boots or gun. He pulled a blanket over himself and began almost at once to snore. Hezzie leaned back, folded her hands, and closed her eyes.

An hour passed. Bill had been sitting quietly, smoking his cigar till it was down to a stub. He got up to put it in the stove, but suddenly sat down again. *"Damn!"* Hezzie opened her eyes. "Is something wrong, sir?"

Bill leaned forward and groaned. Then he straightened up and shouted, "Jack! Get up a minute!"

Jack Burns's eyes opened. "What?"

"I gotta go to the outhouse."

"So why tell me? You had to wake me up for that?"

"I didn't want to leave the old lady."

"Oh, yeah." He sat up on the edge of the bed. "Go on and get back here. I ain't had enough sleep yet."

Bill stumbled out the door. Burns remained on the bed, staring at Hezzie. She had not moved. Burns of a sudden shook himself and looked around as if just realizing where he was. "What's taking that fool so long?" He stood up, then sat down again. "Say, I don't feel so good. You sure you didn't poison that food?"

Hezzie gave a soft smile. "Sir, you watched every ingredient. Potatoes, cabbage, ham. No onions, no poison. Perhaps you have dyspepsia. If you wish, I can brew a soothing tea for the stomach."

"No tea. I think—" He doubled over and moaned.

Bill came back, looking pale and holding his stomach. Burns got up and stumbled past him, heading for the outhouse.

"Probably it's the shock from your wound," Hezzie said. "It has affected your digestion. I can make you a nice stomach poultice ..."

Bill collapsed onto the bed, folding himself in half. "What did you do, you bitch?"

"Why, not a thing. At least, nothing you told me not to. Perhaps, if you are truly ill, I should send for the ambulance?"

"No ambulance." Burns had reappeared in the doorway, pulling up his pants. "You know what would happen."

"At least let me go for help. You two gentlemen both appear ill."

"Yes," Bill said. "I really hurt. Let her go for help. It's you that's got the price on your head, not me."

"Bugger that. It's prob'ly just a bad case of gas. We'll be better by morning. Now get out of that bed, that's mine." Bill groaned again and made no move. Burns grabbed him by one leg and yanked him out onto the floor. Bill screamed. Then Burns whimpered, doubled over, and sat on the bed.

"What has happened to your gun?" Hezzie asked. "You're not wearing it. You must have left it in the outhouse. Would you like me to go and find it for you?" She rose from her chair. Burns stared up at her from the bed, tried to speak and found he couldn't.

As I was saying, my name is Hyram Courtenay. I'm an ordinary merchant in San Francisco. Since Lisbeth and I arrived here we have seen some strange events, among them the fact that I seem to have become one of our wealthiest citizens through no particular effort of my own. But that's beside the point. Sheriff Hays would agree that Hezzie might well join the ranks of strange happenings hereabouts.

When the Sheriff arrived at his office early in the morning, he found Hezzie waiting for him. He asked her kindly what he might do for her. He later told me she did not appear in distress, but rather a bit tired and worn.

She said to him, "Is it true there's a reward out for that Rackety Jack?"

"Yes ma'am, there is. It was put up by the Committee."

"And is it five hundred dollars?"

"Indeed it is."

"I could surely use the money. I need some supplies, and I'll have to purchase a new bed. I wish to claim the reward."

Sheriff Hays sat down behind his desk and lit up a pipe. "Do you now, ma'am? Do you know where this gentleman might be found?"

"Of course. He's in my bed."

Hays blinked and leaned forward as if to hear better. "Come again, ma'am?"

"Rackety Jack is in my bed. Quite deceased, I'm sorry to say."

"Deceased. You mean dead."

"Yes sir. Did the reward say *Dead or Alive?*"

"It was not specified. How did Jack Burns come to be deceased in your bed?

"Oh, by the way, his partner Bill you will find on my floor. He's still alive, far as I know. He might pull through. He didn't eat as much as Mister Burns."

"I see. Well, Miss, as soon as my deputy arrives we'll take a wagon over to your home and see what's what. Aren't you Miss Hezekiah?" Of course a lot of folks in town knew her at least by sight.

She agreed she was, and then sat still, hands folded, as if she had nothing more to say.

After a moment Hays said, "How did Jack Burns come to be dead, Miss?"

"Oh, that. I'm afraid it was the tainted ham. You see, I knew they had no intention of letting me go because I could have told on them. I asked them not to eat the ham, but they did anyway. It was several days old and I knew it was turned. I was only saving it to use for fertilizer in my garden. I could tell by the smell, but I guess their tobacco and cigars prevented them. So I went ahead and fed them dinner. Poor souls never had a chance. When do you think I shall have the reward?"

3

CANDY

J suppose you want to hear another story about the gold rush. Newcomers to this city always do. Please take no offense. I have grown accustomed to telling tales to those who will listen. What comes to mind today is one of the oddest, or my name is not Hyram Courtenay. What reminds me of the story is that piece of candy you're eating. Chocolate, isn't it? I can remember when there was no such thing in California, unless perhaps some of the old Spanish grandees may have hoarded some.

Not that we were entirely bereft of sweet confections. We did have sugar, in limited supplies. You understand, Lisbeth and myself have lived here since San Francisco was called Yerba Buena. There was always plenty of food, and a person might go without clothing or shelter as the Indians often did, since it is rarely too hot or too cold here. But luxuries were often at a premium. Lisbeth took pride in creating miracles of pastry in her kitchen, when there was enough sugar and good flour. But forgive me, now I wander.

The story I am minded of concerns two people, M. Cheval Debruler and his sister, Mme. Ninon Raymon. They arrived as immigrants from France early in 1850. You may have observed since your recent arrival that we have a great many French people here, as well as Germans, Chileans, Australians and what-not. Many of the French arrived here in 1851 because Louis Napoleon kicked them out of prison. Others came because they wanted to get away from Louis Napoleon. All of them, honest or not, hoped to make their fortunes in California.

I'm not sure what inspired Debruler and Raymon to venture forth, but I suspect the hope of riches was involved. I met them as they debarked from the Panama steamer one cold and foggy morning. In fact their ship had been hove to outside the Gate for three days waiting for our fog to lift enough to permit navigation. I often meet ships at the dock as part of my warehousing business, which gives me a chance to size up all of our newest citizens.

M. Debruler spotted me waiting and made a bee line for me. "Sir!" he said. "You appear a respectable citizen!"

I looked him up and down; the man himself did not seem greatly respectable. In fact he looked as if he had not changed or washed his clothing since boarding the steamer. I also glanced around me and realized why his focus had fallen upon myself. There were not many men in business suits on the wharf. I mean, of course, tails and a top hat,

"I suppose I'm about as respectable as we get in this city," I said. "Welcome to San Francisco."

"Thank you, sir." He spoke excellent English, with but a slight accent. I guessed he had studied in Britain. "I am Cheval Debruler," he said. "May I ask to whom I address myself?"

"Hyram Courtenay," I replied, extending a hand. "And I assume this would be Mrs. Debruler?" I smiled at the woman standing behind him.

"Ah, no, m'sieur," he shook his head. "Forgive me for my rudeness. This is my sister, Mme. Ninon Raymon, recently widowed. We wish both to immigrate to California."

I smiled again at the lady, who gave a timid smile and curtsey. She was modestly dressed and had the sort of common face you might forget five minutes after seeing her. I said to her brother, "Well you're here now. Consider yourselves immigrated. Now what can I do for you?"

"Ah. I hoped perhaps you might direct us to a nice hotel, one with rooms for a respectable lady."

"I can do better. I have a buggy. If you don't mind waiting a bit until I complete my business here, I shall escort you to the Hallette House. In the meantime you may want to have a porter collect your baggage."

As it turned out, they had little baggage. I began to understand why Debruler had not changed his clothes. His sister was somewhat tidier, but her dress was well worn.

I saw the two installed in some good rooms at the hotel and took the liberty of inviting them for supper the following day. They seemed eager to accept, and I guessed they both might appreciate a free meal. Since they did not yet know their way around our town I told them I would call for them after my work.

Next evening, Lisbeth prepared a fine supper. In those early days fresh vegetables were sometimes hard to find; potatoes were often unavailable, but we had plenty of preserves put up by Lisbeth herself or by one of her friends. I don't recall now what she served, but I believe it was seafood caught that day.

Debruler proved talkative and Lisbeth encouraged him to hold forth, while I mostly listened. We quickly realized that his sister had little or no English beyond a few common phrases such as Please and Thank you. Throughout the evening she sat quite still with an expression which I can only describe as puzzled, or perhaps lost. I had no way to tell how much, if anything, she understood.

"France is in a sorry state," Debruler was saying. My own attention had wandered. "Louis Napoleon proves himself a tyrant. Peasants starve. There are riots. The Republic, I fear, is lost." I gathered his sister's husband had recently died in some violent disturbance. She had ceased wearing black only about a month ago. Finally Debruler brought the conversation around to what was on his mind. "Perhaps you can tell me something," he asked while Lisbeth was fetching dessert, "of the gold fields?"

I carefully patted my beard with a napkin while attempting to find an answer. Finally I said, "I have not been to the hills myself, sir. As to that, I can only tell what I have heard and what others have told me. Which is, that the fields are a hard life. Not many strike it rich. A few make a living at it. Many come back discouraged and sometimes broken."

He nodded in thought. "If this is so, it is not quite what I expected. I had heard that gold was to be scooped from the ground or taken freely from streams and rivers. Nevertheless, I am determined to make an attempt. I had hoped you might advise me how best to proceed, Mr. Courtenay."

"Go see Sam Brannan," I told him. "You won't have any trouble finding his store. He can sell you an outfit and provide maps of the gold fields and how to get there."

Debruler started to respond, but broke off as Lisbeth served dessert, a sort of Spanish style caramel pudding she had learned from Mexicans. They call it *flan*. Mme. Raymon leaned over to sniff, then took a tiny sample on her tongue. Immediately she burst into a rapid-fire series of French exclamations. Her brother listened. When she stopped he said, "She says this is most excellent. My sister has tasted nothing quite so fine since we left Paris. She begs Madame Courtenay to provide the recipe."

Lisbeth chuckled. "Tell her I'll be happy to write it down, but I'm afraid it will be in English."

"I shall translate," Debruler said.

I tasted the pudding myself and indeed found it fine, and said so. Then a thought occurred to me. I said, "Mr. Debruler, what shall you do with your sister if you go off to the gold country? You can't think of bringing her along, and surely you can't mean to leave her alone here in a strange city."

At this he shrugged, looking embarrassed. "As to that, I had hoped to find her a position. With a glance at his sister, Debruler leaned in my direction and spoke in a low tone. "I hope you will pardon my frankness, m'sieur. I may speak freely since Ninon understands no English. I must tell you she is a good woman, virtuous and hard working. However, she is not what you call *bright*. Ninon permitted her husband to squander his fortune so that now she has nothing. She has no great skills, but she is a fair cook and can always clean floors or wash pots and pans. I hope someone may assist her in my absence."

Lisbeth spoke up. "We have several French restaurants here. Perhaps one of them may need some help."

And so the fate of these two was decided.

About a week later Debruler showed up at our front door one morning as I was about to leave for my warehouse. He wore overalls, a wool shirt and a big grin. "Good morning, sir. I come to say farewell and to beg of M. and Mme. Courtenay to wish me *bonne chance*. I am off to the gold fields to make my fortune."

I looked past him, to observe a large wagon pulled by two mules. It appeared to be loaded to the gunwales with equipment and supplies. "You seem to be well prepared," I said. With Debruler following I went to the gate for a closer look. The wagon looked like it held enough to open a mine. Besides picks, shovels and sluice boxes I noted sacks of flour, bacon and beans.

"M. Brannan assures me I have all I need," he said. "I have also a shotgun and pistol with which to protect myself."

"Indeed. This must have cost you plenty."

He shrugged and grinned again. "You are correct. In fact I am now as you say, *flat broke*. But never mind, I hope to recoup my expenses in a week or so once I reach Sonora."

I turned to shake his hand. "*Bonne chance,*" I said.

We heard no more of M. Debruler for more than a month. Then I found a letter waiting at the post office; it was dated only a week earlier. It said,

· · ·

To my first friends in San Francisco, the Courtenays,
I send you greetings and wish good health. I am well on my way
to making my fortune. At first I had little luck on the river here, but then I
purchased a small claim the previous owners had abandoned. I was forced
to sell much of my equipment to make this purchase. Since then I have
discovered a fresh vein of color and have taken several ounces of dust. I hope
we shall have soon a friendly reunion. Please inquire of my sister, if you
should see her, if she received my letter.

Most sincerely, Cheval Debruler

I showed the note to Lisbeth, who read it with amusement.

"It sounds like our friend has struck it rich," she said. "As a matter of fact, I did drop by the restaurant about a week ago. Ninon is doing well. She has learned some English, and she's been working in the kitchen because they discovered she can make pastries and confections. I believe she's becoming popular. She says she has no wish to be a burden on her brother when he returns from the mines. Tomorrow I will visit her again, and show her this letter."

But as it turned out, Lisbeth couldn't find her the next day. That evening she told me, "I went to the restaurant. They said she moved out two or three days ago. They think she's staying at a rooming house, but they're not sure which one. She said something about 'making her own way,' whatever that means. Tomorrow I'll go into town to make more inquiries."

"I pray she has not fallen in with bad company," I said.

Two or three days later Lisbeth returned from shopping with a broad smile. "I found her," she said. I knew of course whom she meant.

"Where?" I said. Judging by Lisbeth's expression it was no bad place.

"I was walking in the Plaza," she said. Lisbeth meant the block now called Portsmouth Square. "I noticed a small crowd of men and some women huddled in a corner. They appeared to be purchasing something and walking away with happy looks. I approached to discover Madame Raymon with a pushcart. When the crowd thinned I was able to speak to her.

"She has, it seems, managed to rent a room with use of a kitchen. She was saving her earnings from the restaurant. Now she's selling her own candy. Somehow she has found a supply of chocolate. It's much in demand."

"I hope you brought me some," I said. As it turned out, she had brought home the last piece.

I thought no more about Mme. Raymon or M. Debruler for several weeks, except that now and then Lisbeth brought home some newly purchased confections, all of them delicious. Then one afternoon she asked me to accompany her downtown for a "little surprise" as she called it. I put on my coat and tie and brought forth our small buggy. Lisbeth directed me toward the center of town, and we pulled up on a street one block from the Plaza. "Here it is," she said.

At first I saw nothing surprising, until Lisbeth drew me over to a small shop on the corner. There were several men loitering nearby, and it looked to have a steady stream of customers entering and leaving. At first I took it for a saloon. Lisbeth pulled me inside.

"Ah, how delightful to greet you," NinonRaymon said as we entered. She brushed aside three other customers from her counter and brought over a small silver tray. "For you, my freshest candy is always *gratis,* free of charge. Please to sample some."

I did indeed sample a piece of caramel. The aroma inside this shop made my stomach growl. I noticed another girl working behind the counter, selling confections as quickly as she could bring them forth.

"I hope you will admire my new shop," Ninon said. "*La Confectionaire.* The first candy store in this city. C'est delicieuse, non?"

"It is indeed," I said. "You did all this by yourself? From your pushcart earnings?" Lisbeth stood quietly by, looking amused and chewing on something.

"*Oui.* My confections they sell as you say like pancakes. I am most pleased and happy."

My fingers were sticky. I saw no napkins nearby so I was forced to lick them, an act which I must confess I somewhat enjoyed. "I am pleased to see you are doing well. And your brother?" I asked. "Have you heard from him?"

"Indeed. I received a letter from Sonora two days ago. He has struck it rich. By now he will have reached Sacramento. He plans to refresh himself there, to purchase new clothing and convert his dust to coin. Then he returns to San Francisco, perhaps next week."

"How wonderful. Please notify us when he returns. We must have you both over for supper."

"I shall be pleased. But excuse me a moment." A back door had opened and a Chinese boy emerged carrying another tray of confections, apparently fresh from the stove. Ninon seized upon it and began arranging her sweet delights on the counter, where they quickly began to disappear. Seeing how busy she was, Lisbeth and I made our excuses and departed.

You may think that the end of my tale, another story of success and wealth in the gold rush. Almost, but not quite. Nearly three weeks passed before we heard more of Ninon and Cheval. Then I received a note by messenger from Debruler. He had returned to San Francisco, hoped we were well, and wished to see me. I responded with a formal invitation to supper the following Sunday. Lisbeth was delighted, and happy to prepare a roast chicken for the event. She asked me to include a note in my message begging Mme. Raymon to bring one of her fine desserts.

The couple turned up on time, in a hired hack. I seated them in our little parlor to enjoy some of Lisbeth's coffee. Ninon had brought a large box from which some heavenly smell arose.

Now I had a chance to inspect my guests. Ninon, wearing a costly green satin dress, had never looked more radiant. Cheval on the other hand appeared somewhat worse for wear. His clothing looked as if he had worn the same suit for a week. His cheeks were sunken and grey, eyes somewhat bloodshot. I asked him if he were well.

"Ah. As to that, *mon ami,* I have not been well, but I am better since returning to my sister's side. It is well to feel I am needed." Then he made an odd gesture toward his coffee cup. "I beg your pardon, sir. I wonder if perhaps you might have some beverage stronger?"

I smiled at Ninon. "Perhaps Mme. Raymon might like to assist Lisbeth in the kitchen. Our regular cook has Sundays off. Come with me, Mr. Debruler."

I motioned for him to rise, and led him out toward our horse barn. I explained, "Lisbeth does not approve of spirits in the house, but I keep some brandy for special occasions. It's not as good as your cognac, but I hope you will find it not unpleasant." I found the container where I had concealed it a year ago. It was still unopened, and I hoped that age might have improved the bouquet. I poured some into a tin cup. Debruler did not pause to smell, but quickly downed a swallow or two. I refilled his cup.

"I must beg your pardon," he said. "I have been under strains. My luck has not been the best of late."

"Your gold mine—"

He waved a hand, cutting me off. "It is true, what I told in my letters. I had a rich claim. I brought out several thousand dollars worth of dust. But when I reached Sacramento, I fear I fell to human weakness."

I began to understand. "The gambling halls ..."

He shrugged. "The casinos, the ladies of the night, the saloons—I fear I lost it all. But I shall mend my ways. I swear, I shall no longer indulge in such weakness. Not again shall I approach the card tables, nor take strong drink in excess. After all, someone must care for my sister."

He paused to finish the remainder of his cup. I took a sip of my own, offered him more, but he shook his head.

"Thank you for your kindness, *ami.* The truth is, I come today with hopes of begging you for a position. I see I must make my way in an office, or as a common laborer if need be. I thought perhaps you might require assistance for your warehouse."

I considered a moment. "I'm afraid right now I have more workers than I need. But I'm sure I can help you find something else. There are plenty of jobs if you have skills and are not afraid of work. Give me a day or two to make inquiries and I'll contact you next week."

He gave a sweeping, exaggerated bow. "Thank you, m'sieur. This is all that I may ask. I shall be staying for a brief time with my sister, until I can find a house. I thank you again."

We returned to the parlor. The scent of lisbeth's cooking filled the air.

N ow, while you visit our city, you may go down to the French quarter. I think everyone does at last, out of curiosity if nothing else. They have the finest restaurants, as well as theater, music, and of course every vice you may wish for. On the hill over-looking the bay you will find *La Confectionaire*. It is no longer a charming little shop selling candy. It is a regular factory built of brick, employing I am told about fifty souls. Not just Frenchmen, but Italians, Irish, Chinese, even a couple of former slaves from Missouri. The product however is French style chocolate and candies.

I went myself to visit about a month after it opened. It was what you might call a gold mine. Every shop and saloon in this city sells Ninon Raymon confections. Vendors with pushcarts, or just with little trays to carry, purchase from her. I don't know how we ever got along without her.

The occasion of my visit was business. A large consignment of cocoa beans had arrived in my warehouse, and I wanted to find out what Ninon wanted to do with them. She took me on a tour of her factory and I got to sample some of her newest merchandise. She presented me with a basket to bring home to Lisbeth and to our neighborhood ragamuffins. When we were about done, I asked about her brother, M. Debruler.

"Ah." She gave me a smile. "You are in luck, he is working today.

But I have not shown you the scullery. Come, if you would like to say hello."

She led me down a narrow corridor to a room filled with steam from cauldrons of boiling water. She called out, and a man emerged from the mist where several other men and women were working, scrubbing kettles. Debruler gave a bow when he spotted me, while wiping his hands.

"A pleasure to see you, Monsieur Courtenay. I trust you and yours are all well? As you can see, I now assist my sister in managing her company."

"Thank you, we are well." We exchanged a few pleasantries before we shook hands and he returned to work. I noticed his hands were beet red and wrinkled. Ninon led me outside again.

"As you observe," she said, "my brother Cheval is gainfully employed. He has proved useful, and it keeps him occupied." We were standing outside the building now, and she gazed out toward the bay and a departing clipper ship. She spoke in soft tones.

"My brother, you see, is a good man, but not what you would call *bright*. And I fear he has taken up the habit of strong spirits when left too much alone. He squandered his fortune and has nothing."

Ninon turned and gave me a broad smile. She looked quite beautiful that morning. She said, "Cheval does not cook, but at least he is good for cleaning floors, or washing pots and pans."

And she gave me a wink.

GRIZZLY GROGAN

4

HISTORICAL NOTE

*T*his is a work of fiction. All characters are imaginary. However, the wreck of the *San Francisco* and its aftermath occurred as described on February 8, 1854.

My name is Hyram R. Courtenay. I'm not saying what the R stands for because I don't much care for the name. We may have met before. Lisbeth, my wife, and I have lived in San Francisco since it was called Yerba Buena. We never expected to get rich in the warehouse business, but after the Rush started I couldn't keep the cash from flowing in. None of that has anything to do with this story, except as you understand we have been here long enough to witness a lot of strange events. Now I'm going to tell you about Grizzly Grogan.

I'm neither a drinking man, nor a tea totaler. Now and then I might stop by a tavern for a quiet pint when I'm thirsty. That can taste truly good, now they started importing ice from the Russians in Anchorage. I met Grizzly when he was running the show down at the Grizzly Bear, a saloon which was only a block from my warehouse. He was a big man who took no guff, but he was mostly friendly. I did hear he once tossed out a couple of robbers after they threatened him with guns. He took away their pistols, beat them bloody with an axe handle, and told them he'd see them hanged if they didn't leave town. After that his tavern was always peaceful.

One day after a long hot Saturday I dropped in for some refreshment. It was still a bit early for the usual crowd, so just for something to talk about, I asked Grogan how he came to call the place Grizzly Bear.

He wiped his forehead with the same towel he used to dry glasses, and hawked some tobacco juice into a spittoon. "As to that," he said, "it came about because of a little trouble I had on the way west. I fell in with a small wagon train. I didn't have no wagon of my own, just my horse and mule and a few day's supplies. I figured to forage my way across the plains, all the more stupid I was. The Indians lived there all the time, and it were all they could do to forage themselves an indecent living.

"Well, I didn't care for that wagon outfit. They was always fightin' among theirselves. Worse than that, they didn't have no idea how to handle Indians. Now and then a few natives would show up wanting to trade or maybe beg for food. The wagon boss would see them drove off. I figured that wasn't smart since they outnumbered us maybe a thousand to one. After a few days I left the train and went out on my own. Them wagons was traveling too slow to suit me, anyway. You understand, this was over near the Truckee River.

"I guess that was my big mistake. I felt okay because I had my Hawken rifle and Mr Colt's new six shooter with me. A couple days after leaving the wagons, I woke up to find the Northern Paiute stealing my horse and mule. I think they was ten or twelve of 'em. Now, the Paiute are mostly a peaceable tribe, but they musta knowed I was from that wagon train what really had them annoyed. I grabbed my rifle and shot one of them dead. That annoyed 'em even more. They backed off and took cover, but I was in a bad spot. While I was reloading my rifle three or four arrows just missed me.

"I tried shooting with the revolver, but their cover was too good, behind some big rocks. I knew if I stood up they would nail me sure.

What was worse, they had a creek to drink from. I was too far away from it. The sun was up, and it was getting hot and I had no water or food. I knew it was only a matter of time, all they had to do was wait me out and I was a dead man."

Grizzly paused, wiped his brow again, and poured himself a pint of cold ale. He stared off into space for a minute.

"What did you do?" I finally asked him.

"Do? Wasn't nothing I *could* do." He took a fresh plug of tobacco. "I thought of tryin' to wait till dark, then sneakin' off, but I knew they'd probly hear me leaving. Then, all of a sudden, long about early afternoon, I heard the worst commotion you ever did hear. Them injuns started screaming and yelling something fierce. I also could hear a lot of snorting, snarling and grunting. Next thing I knowed, those Paiute were high tailing it out of there. I stood up, thinking of maybe taking a parting shot, then I could see the trouble. The biggest damn grizzly bear what ever lived was chasing them *aba rigunees* back up toward the hills. That bear done saved my life." It took me a moment to realize Grizzly meant aborigines.

He put down his pint and stared into space again. "That's how I come to name this here outfit of mine The Grizzly Bear."

That evening Lisbeth listened quietly to the story as I passed it on, over a dinner of steak and green beans. In those days San Francisco imported most food from places like China, the Sandwich Islands, and South America, so we didn't get much in the way of fresh vegetables. The beans were from our own garden, that's how I recall what we were having. Lisbeth ran the garden these days, but by then we could afford a Chinese cook and a kitchen girl to clean up. I had to admit they did a better job of cooking than Lisbeth ever could, but of course I never said that out loud. Now don't give me *that* look. I know I'm getting off the subject. I'll try to do better.

When I finished the story Lisbeth looked down at her coffee for half a minute, then she sorta grinned. "I know your Grizzly Grogan by reputation," she said. "A number of times down at the general store, I have conversed with ladies who know him well. Not the right sort of ladies, of course. According to what they tell me, he's an entertaining fellow, but a terrible liar."

I considered that. "It's a good story anyway. But what makes you think he's lying? It could have happened."

She stirred some sugar into her coffee. Do you know what they were asking for a pound of sugar in those days? You would be shocked. Oh, *sorry*. Lisbeth took a sip, looked at me, and said, "I just think Grizzly is a bit of a blowhard, that's all."

"Well, I s'pose he is. But then, a fellow is allowed a few weaknesses. I hear he runs a tight ship in his tavern. The rowdies and criminals are terrified of him. He keeps an axe handle behind his bar."

"As far as criminals go, wasn't Mr Grogan arrested for stealing a horse about two years ago?"

"He was," I admitted. "He bribed the jury and got off. "I don't know as he's ever done anything worse."

"Or anything better," Lisbeth said. "Running a tavern of that sort is not what I should call an honorable profession."

I leaned back, wiped my chin, and thought about that. "Well now, you may be correct in that, Lisbeth. But consider now. This city has, I believe, six churches. That's certainly progress, since when we came to this place the only one was the Catholic Mission, and it was all but deserted. Today we have six churches, six pastors and their help, none of them getting rich. But according to the *California Star*, the Christian Association undertook a head count and found we have more than six hundred bartenders. And none of them are poor. It may not be quite honorable, but it's a living."

She laughed. "You do know how to win an argument, Hyram."

I considered some more. "I'm not saying Mr Grogan is an angel. I've no doubt he made off with that horse, and maybe he's done a few other things underhanded. He's been into a few brawls and scrapes, you can tell by his scars. I guess he has lost his temper now and then."

Lisbeth nodded and closed her eyes. When she got that look I always knew she was about to pass some sort of judgment. "It's too bad the man is not married," she said. "I guess there ain't enough good women in this town yet. You men need ladies to calm you down. Men tend to get all emotional, hysterical and panicky. I guess it's what they call your *glands* that does it. You sometimes go off the rail."

I got out my pipe and started loading it with shag cut. Of course I would have to go outside to smoke. I said, "I don't know what I'd come to without you, Lisbeth." She agreed with me.

Then I said, "I always thought he called his place the Grizzly Bear just because someone told him he looks like one." I don't think I mentioned yet that Grizzly had a huge mess of hair on his head and a wiry beard, so his face looked like someone peeking out from a bush. Lisbeth thought that over a second. "Like I said before, Grizzly is a liar."

All that is just to give you some picture of who Grizzly was. He wasn't the worst criminal in town by a long shot, but I wouldn't have trusted him to run a bank. I did not see him again for a couple of weeks, the day of the wreck.

I was down at what we called City Hall in those days, actually a converted musical hall. The city had bought it for ten times its value, but that's another story. I was there to sit in and watch some public hearing by the Board of Aldermen. I don't remember exactly what the hearing was about, something about real estate. Some of us public minded citizens were making it a habit to keep an eye on the Board so maybe they wouldn't steal too much. Half way through the session, someone banged open a side door and yelled, "*There's a wreck!*" The head Alderman banged his gavel and demanded order. The fellow who had run in yelled again, "All Hell's breaking loose!" and ran out again. I decided I had best go see what the commotion was about. The Board was busy declaring itself in recess anyway.

Out in the street, I caught up with a small pack of men all hurrying in the same direction, toward the North Beach, a few blocks away. At the tail end I noticed the fellow who had interrupted the Aldermen. I grabbed his arm. "What's going on?"

He waved in the direction of the bay. "Clipper ship ran aground, over on the north side. They say she's the *San Francisco*."

I had not yet understood. "Why is everyone in a hurry?"

The fellow gave me a grin. "We're headin' for the boats. We're goin' over to do some lootin' and pillagin'." He turned and ran ahead, trying to get to the front of the crowd. Since you're new in town, maybe I should explain here that this city is more law abiding than it used to be, but maybe not as much as London or New York. Lisbeth was right about there not being enough good women to keep us men under control. Most of the time we might conduct ourselves in a reasonably civilized manner, but it did not take much of a push to slide us over into downright folly, if not barbarism.

As a warehouseman, I naturally had an interest in the shipping trade, so I was involved in this crisis whether or no I wished to be. I resolved on the spot to do what I could, if not to mitigate events, at least to witness them. I ran ahead to the beach.

Here I discovered at least fifty men of various sorts engaged in launching boats. These were boats of every description, from two man rowboats to launches, whaleboats, and large fishing boats. By oar and sail they all left the pier and headed out. I myself leaped from the wharf onto a small smack as it passed by. I landed on deck flat on my face but in one piece. I could imagine Lisbeth scolding me for a fool.

There were already about ten men on the boat which was built for a crew of two or three. I looked them over quickly. I have said there was every sort of craft in the water. It appeared there were also every sort of man. Some looked to be downright rascals, dressed in crude and filthy rags. Others wore respectable business attire. One clung stubbornly to his stovepipe hat.

"Where's the wreck?" I asked someone. A man pointed. Then I could make her out, over on the northern shore, just opposite Fort Point. This is the narrowest part of the Golden Gate, entrance to the bay. She was not the first vessel to be wrecked hereabouts, nor the last. In fact I believe we have so far lost twenty or so ships trying to enter or leave the harbor, just in two or three years. The masters are over confident of their navigation, seeing the Gate is more than a mile wide. They sometimes become careless about treacherous rocks.

Two years before, another ship, the *Jenny Lind,* had gone aground in the same place. That was in bad weather, but today the air was clear and free of fog. The breeze was fair, though I could see dark clouds in the west. The Bay was developing a fair chop. Whoever had been on that ship's quarter deck had made one mistake too many.

Suddenly I felt a large hand slap my shoulder. I turned and was startled to find myself staring into the face of Grizzly Grogan. For a moment I thought of bears.

"Come to join in the fun, Hyram?"

"What are you doing here, Mister Grogan?" I could think of nothing else to say, though I was afraid I knew the answer.

"What do you think? It's a chance for clear profit! I mean to take back whatever I can carry!"

"You mean looting." I opened my mouth to berate him on his dishonesty, but then closed it again, knowing it would be of no use. Instead I asked him, "What news do you have? How did you hear of the wreck?"

He grinned, showing his brown snaggle teeth. "News is all over town. The ship has sent up signal flags. They say the passengers and crew are all safe and the cargo's intact, but she's hard aground. A fat plum ripe for picking."

"I see. What about the agents? Haven't they sent someone to take charge?"

He gave a loud laugh. "And where might their army be found?"

I was quickly resigning myself to the worst. It would obviously do no good to lecture this crowd on lawlessness. Most of them carried guns or Bowie knives or both. Grogan had moved up to the bow, as if anxious to be first off the boat. As we grew closer I could make out more details of the clipper. It appeared the crew had remained on board long enough to cut the lines to her sails, which were now flapping in the wind. That would reduce the risk of her hauling off the beach and sinking. Steep cliffs rose on all sides, but the beach was level and sandy. It would be easy to land boats there. Soon enough we arrived, along with a number of other small craft. The smack came to a halt in sand. The skipper quickly dropped his sail while the men aboard leaped ashore. I was last off.

Here I witnessed a scene of chaos and anarchy of the worst sort. All the ship's hatches were open, and already goods and crates of various kind were being tossed overboard onto the beach. The *San Francisco* leaned heavily to her port side, over the sand. This made it easy to get cargo out onto the ground. The ship's crew had left a scrambling net over the rail when they evacuated. This of course made it easy to board. Ripe for picking indeed. Already I could count a dozen small boats beached nearby, many of them half loaded.

I noticed a small knot of men standing together further back on the beach, merely watching. Most of them wore business clothes, a few in marine attire. I went over to them and tipped my hat.

"Would one of you gentlemen be this ship's agent?"

A burly fellow stepped forward. "I'm Schimmerhorn. I represent the company. Who might you be?" He spoke with a German accent. As you probably know, our city has a large German community, including prominent citizens. I remembered this man's face at some of the Aldermen's council meetings. I gave him what I hoped was a friendly smile and gestured toward the scene behind me.

"This is truly a disgrace, isn't it? The army should be here to restore order."

One of the other men spat in the sand. "We no sooner got the crew and passengers safely off this beach than this rabble started showing up. There's too many of them to handle."

Another fellow, this with a grand waxed mustache, favored me with a scowl. "I'm O'Sullivan, insurance agent. This is a bad business. The cargo is covered for loss at sea, but not for theft."

I gave them my name. "They may take some of your goods to my warehouse for storage. If you can identify any of it, it's yours."

The German flopped down heavily in the sand. "We will come and look, but it's not likely. What they can't use they will probably sell at once. There is a good variety—furniture, tools, mining equipment, clothing, medicine, preserved foodstuffs ..." He broke off, staring past me at something on the ship. I turned to look. Several men were attempting to wrestle an upright piano out of one of the hatches. I wondered how they hoped to get it aboard their boat.

Just then another man in our group pointed and said in an excited voice, "*Look!* The Army has arrived!"

I turned in time to see a small launch run headlong into the sand. Nine or ten men in uniform piled out. For a moment I felt delight, until I realized none of them carried weapons. Nor was there an officer among them. They headed straight for the pile of goods on the beach and began carrying them back to their boat. I looked at the ship's agents. None of them spoke or made a move. What was the use?

Just then I noticed Grizzly Grogan heading across the beach toward the boat he'd arrived in. He carried a large bundle over one shoulder. He saw me and grinned, and I thought not of a bear, but rather of some old time pirate, Edward Teach perhaps, with the flaming matches in his beard and a dagger between teeth. "What have you got there?" I asked.

"Enough opium to buy City Hall!" He laughed, hefted his bag, and kept going. By now the mob of looters had increased to what looked like two hundred men. Some of them began fighting between themselves over some item of swag or other. I fully expected to see shots exchanged or knives bloodied.

To understand what happened next, you should know something of our weather here. The Bay can be cold and foggy in the middle of summer, or warm and sunny in December, depending on the whims of the gods. Or it may be warm in one place while drizzly and damp two miles away. And it can change from one condition to another in the blink of an eye.

The German sat on the sand, legs apart, an unlit cigar clamped in his jaws. A man next to him, in sailor's garb, pointed out to sea. "That's a squall line," he said.

A few minutes later the looters on the beach began to point as well. Most of their boats were already loaded to the gunwales. One by one they began pushing their craft into the water. I could see we were in for a drenching. By now it was late afternoon, the *San Francisco* having run aground early that morning. I turned to one of the sailors near me to ask how long he thought the rain might last. I should not be fond of spending the night in the open in pouring rain; that might be a guarantee of pneumonia. By the time I had got my question ready in my mouth, the man and several others were gone. There were three sailors in our group; they and two other men were already on the scrambling net, headed for the deck of the clipper. For a moment I wondered if they expected to take shelter in the foundered ship. But a few minutes later they were throwing spars and sailcloth over the side. By the time the rain reached our position they had already thrown up a lean-to, under which we all huddled. Someone else had gathered dry driftwood from further up the beach and was making a fire.

Now, all this had taken little time, not more than half an hour. Meanwhile some of the looters were still gathering goods from the pile on the beach and loading their boats. The last of them shoved off just as the squall hit. I resigned myself to a cold night at the shore; it would take hours before a rescue boat might arrive to take us off. I huddled in a corner of the makeshift tent, wishing for dinner and regretting I had left home at all that day. Then one of the sailors gave a shout and pointed.

"Mister Simmons! They are lost!" By his manner of address I guessed the other sailor must be the mate or another officer. I got to my feet and looked to see what had their attention. Off the point, a hundred or so yards out, I could see an overturned whaleboat. Its crew were nowhere to be seen.

"And there!" Mr Simmons pointed in another direction. A launch, heavily loaded, was going down by the bow. Some of the men aboard were in the water, struggling toward shore.

"The tide's running out," someone said. "Look, some of those boats are being swept to sea."

I was horrified, cold and helpless. With the rain, the wind had risen and whitecaps towered in ten foot waves. It would be suicide to attempt rescue in a small boat, even if we had one. I estimated there were at least fifty looters still in sight; I was watching them drown before my eyes. Lightning flashed, with thunder a second later.

"Serves them right," O'Sullivan the insurance agent said. He spat tobacco into the sand. "Divine retribution, is what I calls it."

A few of the looters were able to make it back to shore, but mostly without their loot. Some of them had tossed all their goods overboard to keep from sinking. Some others swam ashore by holding on to floating crates or barrels. We did not exactly welcome them, but we did allow a few to share our tent and fire.

That night was long. The rain squall relented about an hour after it had begun, to be replaced by bitter cold. Most of the goods remaining on the beach were by that time ruined. When dawn finally arrived, I could see the upright piano still on the ship, where it had slid down the deck to be stopped by the port rail. I wondered what fine tune it might play now.

I had looked for Grizzly Grogan, hoping to see him alive. I didn't know if he could swim or knew anything of handling boats. No doubt he deserved what he had got, but then again I had known worse men than him. There was no sign. A tugboat arrived in the morning to take us off the beach. There were only guesses about the number of drowned. The consensus was about a dozen. Some had survived by throwing all their stolen goods in the sea and staying with their boats. Others had not the chance, being overturned in the first gust of wind. By the time I got home Lisbeth had already heard the story from a neighbor. She made no comment, did not scold, but merely served me hot soup.

Of course I assumed I should not meet with Grizzly again. A few days after the disaster I happened to stroll past his saloon. It was boarded up with a For Sale sign in front. How the mighty have fallen, I thought. Man proposes, God disposes. Grizzly Grogan would be asleep in the deep, down with Davey Jones and his ill-gotten goods. I heard later that the *San Francisco* and her remaining cargo were auctioned for twelve thousand dollars. Before the wreck she would have been valued at about four hundred thousand. A month or so after the wreck, Grizzly had all but slipped from my memory when, as Lisbeth and I were on our way out of church, a hand like a bear's paw clamped upon my shoulder.

"Mister Court'nay!" a man bellowed in my ear. I staggered, in fear of being under attack.

"It's me! *Grizzly!*"

I gaped at him. He was a large man with a florid red face and a huge grin. No sign of a beard or hair. It was a face I had never seen before. He whipped off his cap. "See! I'm bald now!" His scalp, like his face, was clean shaven. "And this must be yer missus Lisbeth!" He gave a deep bow. "I'm right pleased to meetcha, ma'am. This here is my new wife, Sunflower!" His arm reached behind and swept forward a small woman. She had Indian features, with jet black hair tied in a braid and equally black eyes. She regarded us without expression.

"Sunflower's not from around here," Grizzly explained. "She ain't one of yer Digger injuns. She's Navajo, real civilized. She told me she wouldn't marry me less'n I shaved and got a haircut."

Lisbeth gave a curtsey. "I'm pleased, Missus Grogan." Sunflower stared at her.

I started to ask Grizzly how he had survived drowning, but he didn't wait for the question. "It were all because of that there storm. You remember that, don't you, you were there and all?" I agreed that indeed I remembered.

"It done changed my life. I got swept off the deck of that boat right away. Can't swim, neither. I was sure it was all up for me. I done said my final prayers to the Almighty and promised if he got me out of that fix I'd try to do better with my life. Then I grabbed onto a floating box that kept my head out of the water. At the time I couldn't figure why that box didn't sink to the bottom with all the rest. Turned out, when I got to shore, it was a box full of wine corks. I figured right then it was what they call Divine Intervention.

"I washed up on the south shore, not far from the fort. I guess I woulda froze except I made it to the army post where they had a fire. I swore right then and there I'd change my ways and keep my promise to Almighty. No more lootin', pillagin', lyin' or fightin'. A few days after that I met Sunflower here. She had somehow got hooked up with a wagon train headed for California. You might say we both washed ashore at the same time. She don't talk much English yet, so I haven't got her whole story or why she left Arizona Territory. But she was so beautiful I asked her right off if she wanted to marry me. She said yes. Now this lady here is the light of me life and I does love her dearly. I guess I'm right lucky."

"And you have joined the church, I see." He was wearing what might pass for a respectable Sunday suit, though a bit threadbare.

He nodded vigorously. "Joined a church and the Temperance Union. Me and strong drink have met a partin' of the ways. I got me a job at a dairy farm, milkin' cows and such, so I don't get to town too often. That's prob'ly a good thing, keeps me away from temptations of the flesh."

Sunflower was tugging at his sleeve. "We go now. Enough talk."

He grinned. "Sure, my dear. We go now." He gave me a wink. "Keeps me on the straight, she does. Be seein' you, Mister Court'nay." And they were off. I watched until they boarded a small surrey. He snapped the reins and they rode away. I haven't seen them since.

Lisbeth gave me one of her looks. This one meant, "What did I tell you?"

It was the damnedest thing. By now I ought to be used to the damnedest things in this city. I favored Lisbeth with a low bow. "You were right once more," I told her. "All he needed was the right woman." And, I thought to myself, a little Divine Intervention. And a box full of corks.

FARO

5

SAN FRANCISCO, 1851

*L*et me tell you about Faro Dawkins. I don't expect that was his real name. Lots of men end up here in San Francisco with new names they never had before, or sometimes with no names at all. Women too, I guess. This particular fellow was called Faro because he gambled. You might say he made his living that way.

I'm Hyram Courtenay. You may remember me. I run a warehouse here. Somehow I have become one of the city's leading citizens, without half trying. Lisbeth and I have lived here since before the gold rush. I met Mr Dawkins because I made the mistake of getting myself elected to the Board of Aldermen. Among my other underpaid duties was that of organizing our various fire companies.

One day Max Helle, Chief of the Phoenix Fire Company, came to see me at my warehouse. As usual he was chewing an old cigar butt. He leaned against a doorway and talked around the butt. "You have to approve something," he said.

I gave him a smile. "Whatever it is, you'll do it anyway if you want to, approval or not. What is it this time?" I might explain, we had by this time four different fire companies, all independent and all competing to be the best in the city. I expected Max was going to petition for a grant to buy more equipment.

"New recruit," he said. "Judge Dawkins found this futilitarian guilty of being a nuisance. The judge is his uncle. He gave him a choice of jail or volunteering to join the company. An alderman has to sign off on the deal."

I scratched my head. This was something new, at least I'd never heard of it. But then there was always something new in this town. "Who is it? And where is he?"

"Name of Faro. He's outside." Max led me out the door, where we found a tall young fellow leaning against a wall. He had a dapper appearance, with a neatly waxed mustache and wearing a natty jacket and vest. When he saw me he straightened up, gave a quick bow, and winked. "How d'ya do, Mister Courtenay. I'm pleased."

"You would be Faro," I said, giving him a once over.

"The very same. Faro Dawkins at your service. The one what Judge Dawkins has it in for."

Max elbowed me. "He caused a near riot in the card room other night. Caught cheating."

"Slander and libel," Faro responded. "Judge Morgan was losing fair and square. I never cheated in my life." This statement was followed by another wink.

I said, "I am told you wish to join a fire company."

He shrugged. "Better than the chain gang, I guess."

"I'm not so sure. Very well, if you're willing to train and work, I'll approve. Max here will report back to me. If you're found shirking, it's back to jail for you."

He grinned. "Work's my middle name." That was Faro's beginning with the fire company.

∾

I guess you're new in town. They tell me you're from the States, Pennsylvania or some such. You weren't here when we had the fires. The one back the previous May had wiped out most of downtown. Faro showed up in late May. We were still rebuilding then, but we were coming along. That was before the fire a month later that nearly destroyed us again. We have had six great fires in this town, in a little over three years. But please don't concern yourself, it will never happen again. We have good fire companies and a lot of cisterns. San Francisco will never again have a great fire of such magnitude.

Well, here I'm getting ahead of myself. I was only going to tell you about Faro. I guess San Francisco comes up with some of the strangest characters on this planet. Some people think there might be folks living on the Moon. I know some who would fit right in there.

I got most of the story later on, from talking to Max. Faro joined up with the Phoenix Fire Company all right. Their house was down near the foot of Mission Street, near the waterfront. Most of the other firemen didn't take much to Faro. They were all volunteers. He was the only conscript. If his uncle hadn't been a judge he would have been serving time in jail. As it was, he was on three weeks probation, so we all expected he would leave the company after doing his time. The company did make him get some training, though. They assigned him as a hook man, that being about the most dangerous job for a fireman.

This was a hook and ladder company, you see. But I guess you don't know much about fire fighting. The thing is, when a house is on fire sometimes the only way to get a handle on it is to tear down the walls. The firemen haul a big wagon full of ladders and hooks, as well as axes and other tools. Sometimes the ladders are used to rescue people from upper floors. More often, a man has to go up, chop a hole in a wall and then use one of the hooks to try to pull the wall down. No job for a coward.

Faro was spending half his time at the company, cleaning equipment and sweeping out the fire house. What spare time he had left, he'd go on down to the gambling houses where he'd deal Monte or Faro, or sometimes play that new game, Poker. I guess he brought in enough cash doing that. He didn't get paid for fighting fires.

And he did get involved in a few small fires. At first the company had two or three little hand pumps. When a house caught fire, they'd hook up to a cistern or whatever water was around and start pumping. Then, one day the Hanuman arrived.

I was there when they brought it off the ship. As warehouseman I usually made it my business to be on hand when any cargo offloaded from a new ship at the wharf. The Hanuman had been ordered by Max Helle himself, a year earlier. It was built by the Hanuman engine company back in Boston, and came around the Horn. When news of its arrival came, the entire Phoenix company showed up at the dock to witness its uncrating. Of course Faro was there as well. In fact Max made him do most of the hard work with a crowbar, prying off boards. The thing was huge, a good ten feet long. The rest of the company stood by and watched while Faro hammered and pried.

Finally it was done. The brand new fire engine stood revealed, shining under the sun. Faro dropped his tools, stepped backward two paces and just stared. It was beautiful, red with jet black pump handles and gold and silver trim. A red lantern hung at each end and a great silver bell swung from a frame in the center.

For about a minute no one said anything. A couple of the boys walked slowly half way around, saying not a word. Someone gave a low whistle. Other than some of the special ladies downtown, it was probably the loveliest object any of them had yet seen in San Francisco.

Finally Faro turned to Max. He said, "Can I help pull her?"

I guess that was the beginning of Faro's life as a fireman. Before that he'd been a card sharp pretending to be a part time fire fighter. With that Hanuman in the house, he began spending more of his free time at the company. He spent some of that time getting the other boys to play cards, and winning money from them more often than not. I don't doubt he did some cheating. On the other hand he was smart enough to not win all the time. On balance he won more than he lost, or so Max told me later. The other boys didn't seem to mind.

He also put in some hard work oiling and polishing that Hanuman engine. The company put in some practice with it, but it didn't require much in the way of training. One end had a siphon hose that would go into a cistern or any other water source. Four men on each side would handle the pump levers, but it would work with only two men if necessary. Another fireman would man the hose. The machine also had a reservoir that held about fifty gallons, in case there was no cistern nearby. Manning the pump was hard work, but even worse was hauling that engine up one of our hills.

They got a chance to try it out about a week after its arrival. We had a hotel fire over on Powell Street. The signal bell started clanging and the Phoenix company rolled out, along with two other nearby companies, I misremember which ones. Some citizens noticed what trouble the boys were having hauling their Hanuman uphill, so they pitched in to help. There must have been a good twenty men pulling that machine by the time it arrived at the fire. Everyone in town was nervous about fires because they could remember the big one we'd had three weeks before.

The Phoenix Company did itself proud that day. The hotel had three stories. In no time, the company had ladders up and began pulling down the walls. It was the engine's first big fire. It was also Faro's first real fire. He was in there with the veterans, with axe and hook. Others were pumping the Hanuman, throwing water. By the time it was over, that hotel was a smoldering pile. Two of the former guests got burned and one died, but about forty others were saved. No firemen were hurt. Most important, the fire didn't spread. When the men got back to their fire house, Max Helle bought them all a big keg of lager.

Someone noticed that Faro had changed. Not just what he did, but how he looked. When he'd first arrived in the company he had been a regular dandy. Now he didn't seem to pay much attention to his clothes except when he was in uniform, which I must say looked rather elegant on him, with the striped shirt and leather helmet. His muscles were getting harder, if not bigger. And he let his mustache grow. You ever wonder why firemen all have bushy mustaches? It's to help them breathe when they're in smoke. They get them wet and try to breathe through the hair. They say it helps. Faro finished out his three week's probation and he could have gone back to playing cards full time, but he chose not to. He stayed with the company. He still went down to the card room now and then, but he wasn't spending a lot of time there. At first he'd devoted his life to the cards and only went to the fire house because he had to. Now it was the other way around, at least that's how it looked.

My wife Lisbeth got to meet Faro. That was during one of my regular inspections of the fire companies, which I did about once a month. The visits were supposed to be good for morale; as alderman I had neither the authority of discipline should I find anything wrong, nor the ability to offer rewards for virtue. Now and then I might attempt to pry some cash out of the city corporation for more equipment or salaries, but I never had much success in that, at least not until after the last fire.

When I introduced Lisbeth to the Phoenix Company, they as usual applauded. They were always happy to see her, as she always brought cookies. Faro stepped forward and gave a deep bow, sweeping his helmet from his head. He looked elegant. I noticed he'd even gone to the effort of having his trousers pressed and creased, something unheard of for a fireman.

"Ma'am," he announced, standing straight. "Being new here, I have not had the pleasure of your acquaintance. I present myself as the newest and greenest of this illustrious fire company. Faro Dawkins, the name."

Lisbeth smiled and gave a curtsey. "And I have heard much about you, Mister Dawkins. I'm told you show great promise."

"Well, as to that, ma'am, I'll promise you anything in exchange for one of your cookies."

Lisbeth laughed. "And that is one bargain I find agreeable." She handed him the whole box. Behind Faro the other men were grinning. One of them shouted, "That's one cookie, Faro! You don't keep the box!"

Faro grinned and began passing out cookies.

The main event of this inspection was the Hanuman engine. The company hauled it out in the street so the neighborhood could watch. A number of small children gathered around, wide eyed. The Hanuman had been polished so her bell and gold trim shone like the sun, and her red paint was like Chinese Lacquer. The engine's reservoir had been filled. There were a total of nine men in the company besides Chief Helle. Four men on each side manned the pump levers, while another played out the hose. At Helle's signal the men pumped. At first nothing happened, though I could hear a hiss of air. Then, on the third or fourth stroke, there was a sudden spurt and then a gush of water. The hose shot water a hundred feet or so down the road; most of the small boys in the audience raced to get drenched under the spray. The hose man lowered the nozzle and managed to knock some of the boys rolling, screaming, off their feet. They got up immediately and rushed back to the water.

It was over in a few minutes. The tank ran dry, the stream failed and the men were pumping air. The men stopped, red-faced and sweating under their helmets.

"Thank you, men," Max said. "That was well done. You may replace your equipment." He turned to me. "If we were close to a cistern, or maybe Mission Creek, we could pump water all day. It's easy to pump once she gets started."

"A fine looking engine," I agreed. "I only wish the city had more like them."

Later, in our carriage, Lisbeth leaned close to me so our driver wouldn't hear. She said, "Men do enjoy having a large hose, don't they?"

～

Then June the twenty second arrived. Perhaps I have already explained that the city was still recovering from the last big fire. A large portion of the business area had already burned. Some men lost everything. Instead of complaining they began to rebuild. Some new buildings were put together in as little as ten days. There were also plans for more fireproof structures, but those would take more time. Most people believed the fires were started by incendiaries, what some call "fire bugs." We still had many undesirables in town, some of them straight from the penal colonies in Australia. No doubt that nation was happy to get rid of them. A few criminals made it a hobby to set fire to buildings as a distraction, so that they might enter and rob the house next door. Such miscreants were hard to find and harder to catch, but when they were, they were usually hanged at once.

The evening of the twenty first I had by coincidence run into Max Helle at City Hall. I inquired how Faro Dawkins was getting along. Max laughed, shaking his head. "That depends who you ask. He'd probably say he's getting along just fine. He hasn't been a fireman for long, but he seems to enjoy working at it. He also enjoys getting the other men into card games and taking their money. Some of them would like him to go away. I must say he's the slickest card sharp I ever met."

At about eleven in the morning of the next day, on the twenty second, a fire started at the corner of Pacific and Powell streets. There was a high wind that morning, and there had been no rain since April. One of our fire companies got there quickly, but the cistern ran dry while the fire raged and spread. The alarm bell continued ringing, until every company in the city converged on the area. Before we knew it we had another great fire to fight.

Many of the local merchants had been through this before. They quickly began moving goods and possessions to the Plaza, which soon became crowded with people and their freight. Later, their efforts proved useless as the fire spread to piled furniture and boxes.

My own house lay on the outskirts of town. I was not greatly concerned about my own property, since my warehouse was even further, in Mission Bay. By this time I did own some other properties in the city, but I could withstand their loss. Today was Sunday, so I had not gone to work. When I heard the alarm bells I asked Lisbeth to secure the house as well as possible, filling every bucket with water just in case. Then I hurried to the scene of conflagration.

By the time I arrived it was a picture of nearly total chaos. Smoke was everywhere. Already there were loud explosions, buildings being demolished with black powder. I wet my bandanna and held it over my mouth, the better to breathe. Citizens were running everywhere, some of them carrying goods on their backs, others with buckets in hand.

One man, running full tilt away from the fire, stopped near me, panting and gasping. I asked if he was all right.

"Got to get away," he choked out. "There's a store back there full of black powder!" Then he began to run again. I didn't know whether to believe him or not. I didn't suppose there was much I could do to help, but I looked for some firemen. It wasn't long before I crossed paths with the Phoenix company. Two men were pulling their engine away from the fire, while others hammered at a nearby store front with axes.

"What are we doing here?" I asked a man with the engine.

"What's it look like? We need to find some water. This is no good." He pulled and heaved. I got behind the engine and pushed. There was a loud crash behind me and I looked around to see the store front topple to the ground. A couple of the men left it and ran to help with the engine. One of them was Faro Dawkins.

"Where is Chief Helle?" I asked him. He pointed back toward the fire.

"In the thick of it. It's the damndest thing. I even saw the mayor awhile ago. He was arguing with the chief of another company. He told the chief to tear down a building. The chief said he wouldn't do it because it belonged to the mayor himself. The mayor grabbed an axe and started chopping. That building came right down."

"You think we can stop this fire?" I asked.

Faro shrugged and grinned. "I dunno, but we'll sure give it hell." I wondered if he meant Helle.

The conflagration raged all night and into the next day before being controlled. In the end we had lost ten square blocks totally destroyed, with damage to another six. Fortunately the main business section was this time spared. We did lose City Hall, and the Jenny

Lind Theatre burned for the third time. Oh well, that was months ago now. We are fast rebuilding, with more reservoirs and some fire proof buildings, with walls of masonry two feet thick and iron shutters. San Francisco, I am sure, will never see another great fire.

As to Faro, I learned of his fate from Chief Helle, some time later. After a few hours sleep I went to visit the Phoenix company fire house. The Hanuman engine was parked in front, being cleaned and serviced by two firemen. The Chief came over when he saw me watching. "She'll need some repainting, and we'll have to replace some of the gold trim. But she saw good service, if we did run low on water."

"I'm glad to see you could save the engine," I told him. "What of the men? Any injuries?"

His face became grave. "Most of them not serious. Except for Faro Dawkins. I'm afraid he's lost."

I was stunned, and could not speak for a moment. Then I asked, "The fire—"

He shook his head, apparently having been away in thought a moment. "No, it was not the fire. It was a man. Faro was busy pulling down a wall when he spotted a man running. The man held a torch. Obviously an incendiary. Faro grabbed an axe and took off after him. As he caught up to him, the fellow turned and fired a pistol. Faro buried his axe in the man's head." He stopped, as if having difficulty speaking.

"And then ..."

Max gave a shrug. "We got Faro back to the firehouse, lying on the engine. We couldn't find a doctor, but I don't know that it would have made a difference. We couldn't stop his bleeding."

I did not know what to say. Finally Max looked up at me. "You want to know his last words? He said, *We sure gave that fire hell.* You might say the Hanuman was baptized in his blood. We're going to give Faro a good send off. I already put the notice in three different newspapers. Not the *Alta California,* though. That paper burned down."

So that's Faro's story. I guess he won't be remembered a hundred years from now, but the boys in the firehouse still tell stories about him. They yet believe he cheated them all at cards, but they could never prove it. His funeral was three days after the fire. A lot of folks read about his stopping the firebug, and how he helped to save the engine. About two thousand people turned out to follow him to the graveyard. Myself, I chose not to go, but stood on the sidelines and doffed my hat as the black carriage passed.

Some stranger came up to me, someone I guess who had not heard the story. He asked me whose funeral this was, assuming it must be someone important. I turned to him when the wagon had passed, replaced my hat, and proceeded to light my pipe.

"Just a card sharp," I told him. "The slickest card sharp you might ever meet."

6

A LIGHT WILL SHINE

San Francisco, 1855

> The Lighthouse on Alcatrazes or Bird Island, mounted
> the new Fresnel light for the first time last evening. It
> burns brilliantly, and in fine weather can be seen at a dis-
> tance of twelve miles out at sea. The light is at an ele-
> vation of 160 feet above the level of the sea.
> The coast of California has long suffered for the want of
> proper lighthouses, which, had they been constructed,
> vast amounts of property would in all probability not have
> been destroyed. Vessels of all classes, from steamers
> down to the smallest craft, have been lost on this coast
> when proper beacons would have directed them safely into
> a harbor.

Trefry Micarden was quite mad. I'm convinced of that now, though at the time I had my doubts. The truth is, we all fear darkness, and I failed to see it in him. We are all flashes in this infinite night.

I met Mr. Micarden's wife Hallette before I ever heard of him. In San Francisco we do sometimes see women traveling alone, but they are not usually of the proper sort. Hallette Micarden was her own species, like her husband. Oh, but forgive me, I forgot for a moment we had not been introduced. This saloon has good beer and spirits, but it sometimes causes me to forget formalities. I am Hyram Courtenay, warehouseman and long time resident of this strange city at the edge of a boundless sea.

Mrs. Micarden showed up one day at my place of business, just after I opened the door in the morning. I'm afraid I gave her a second look, since we rarely if ever have ladies show up at my warehouse. She was well but conservatively dressed in an outfit I guessed was purchased back east, judging by its good quality. Like her clothing, I took the lady to be of quality as well.

"You would be Mr. Courtenay?" she asked after I had shown her to my small office.

"Yes, ma'am. May I ask whom I am addressing?"

She told me her name. "I'm sorry to have to meet you without benefit of formal introduction, but I have just arrived in your city. I have come in on the *California*. I know no one here, and there was no time for propriety. Your name was given to me by a merchant in New York, a Mr. Cavendish."

"Of course, I remember the gentleman. May I ask how was your journey? Have you found proper quarters? You may have heard rumors that San Francisco is a difficult place for respectable ladies. I'm afraid the rumors are largely correct."

"I have taken rooms at the Rassette house," she said. "I have heard this is your best hotel."

I nearly told her it was our *only* hotel, if you mean respectable establishments. I refrained. I was about to inquire what had brought her to my office, but she withdrew a small packet from her reticule.

She said, "The worst part of my journey was navigating your muddy streets. Please read this letter. It will explain why I am here."

I broke the seal and unfolded the paper. I glanced at the bottom, noting it was signed by Mr. Trefry Micarden. I might say that until that moment I was unsure if Mrs. Micarden was actually a married lady. Many women of the lower classes and professions arrive here with Mrs. in front of their names to disguise their real status.

After reading the letter twice I looked up at her, sitting with folded hands and awaiting my response. "I must say your husband has an unusual name. Would that be from the French?"

She gave an impatient shrug. "Cornish."

"I see. This letter says you wish to reserve a secure storage space, fire proof and water tight, with barricaded doors. You also wish to hire the service of armed guards after a certain item arrives by sea and is deposited here."

"Yes." She gave a quick nod. "Are you able to satisfy these requirements?"

"Certainly," I said, after thinking a few seconds. "I have an old adobe structure formerly used for storage of cured meats. I can easily reinforce the door. As for the guards, they should not be difficult to arrange if you can pay for the muskets and powder."

At this Mrs. Micarden gave a brief smile, the first time I had noted this expression on her. "Easily. This document should be sufficient to establish our credit." She handed me another paper, this one a letter of mark drawn on a prominent eastern bank.

I looked it over. "I'm usually paid with gold or silver, but I shall be happy to retain this as collateral. May I inquire what sort of item ..."

She shook her head. "I'm afraid not. We prefer this remain secret until the time comes. Mr. Micarden is aboard a sailing ship at present, bound around the Horn. With any luck they have by now reached the Pacific. He accompanies an extremely rare and valuable item. We prefer no one hear of it until the proper time."

"I understand. However, this is an unusual request. If I am to satisfy your requirements, I should have some idea what sort of—"

"I can give you one hint," she said. Again the faint smile. "My husband is employed by the Lighthouse Service."

Mrs. Micarden again visited a week later, this time giving me fair warning by way of messenger. Knowing what she wanted, I had a buggy waiting to convey us the few blocks to my storage room. Once there she wasted no time in dismounting and inspecting the place.

"As you can see," I told her, "I have reinforced the door with oaken beams and iron straps. It needs only a good lock. There are no windows, and the roof is Spanish tile, watertight."

She spent a few minutes looking around. There was nothing inside the small building save an earthen floor. "This should be adequate," she finally pronounced. "Although it's barely large enough."

I was puzzled. "You said there is only one item ..."

"I did. However, I'm afraid I failed to mention the item is disassembled and in several crates. Actually, there are three separate items, closely related. They are rare and expensive. We are taking no chances on theft or vandalism."

"I understand. When you're ready, I plan to hire three men I trust as guards. They are Kanakas and will brook no nonsense. I have used them before to guard gold shipments."

She nodded. "Excellent." Then she gazed into space a moment, her eyes distant. "By my figuring, Mr. Micarden's ship should be near Chile by now. Perhaps it's in Valparaiso, restocking provisions."

I had the odd feeling that Mrs. Micarden could see her distant husband, like some crystal gazer.

That evening I discussed the matter with my wife Lisbeth over supper. Also dining with us was Jimmy Bagley, a boy I had recently hired to sweep up. Mrs. Micarden had told me to keep her business confidential, but since she had revealed practically nothing I had few qualms.

"Lighthouse service?" Jimmy perked up when I mentioned it. Jimmy was one of those boys who seemed to appear in town from time to time, without parents, relatives or antecedents. They seemed somehow to survive. Jimmy came around looking for work, and as it happened I had some for him.

"What's the Lighthouse Service?" he asked.

"Something new," I told him. "They're taking over some duties from the Coast Guard. The U.S. government is putting up money for a chain of lighthouses along the coast, from Mexico to Canada. As I heard it, San Francisco is first because of our port."

"Wow. I'd like to work in a lighthouse. Where do you s'pose they'll put it?"

I had to shrug. "I heard there might be more than one. Where, I couldn't say."

Lisbeth put some more mashed potatoes on Jimmy's plate. She said, "There was an item in the *Alta* yesterday, you must have missed it. They're going to put the first light on Bird Island."

"Or Alcatraz, as we call it now. That makes sense. A ship coming through the Gate at night could get her bearings and avoid the cliffs. We have had too many ship wrecks there."

"Mr. Micarden must be involved in building that light," Lisbeth said. "I suppose he's some sort of engineer."

I turned to Jimmy. "I don't think you'd care to live there. It's a barren rock, the only thing there now is the Army prison. They have to haul all their water in on a barge. Not much to do for amusement, I'd say."

Jimmy looked thoughtful. "It still might be fun, though. What with a big light like that to shine on stuff."

Lisbeth laughed. "It might be fun at that, Jimmy."

About two weeks later I had another visit from Mrs. Micarden. I had been hearing occasional rumors about her; it seems she was often seen at the Mechanic's Institute, a rare place for a woman, accompanied or not. She had been observed poring over maps, charts, and geological survey reports. She also often visited the Long Wharf, where she was heard to enquire of arriving sea captains possible news of her husband's ship. She showed up at my warehouse, as before, just after I had opened for business that day.

"There has been a sighting," she said without preamble.

"I beg your pardon?" I put down my pipe which I had been about to light.

"My husband's ship, the *Oriole*. A fast coasting schooner has arrived here from Valparaiso. They report hailing her north of Panama. She should arrive here in another week or so. Thank God, it has been a quick passage."

I wasn't sure how long that ship had been at sea, but if it was less than five months it would indeed be quick.

"I wish to inspect your storage room again, if you please. I'm sorry if it's a bother, but—"

I waved a hand. "No bother at all, I quite understand. Give me a few minutes to speak to my foreman."

Mrs. Micarden had arrived in a rented hack which waited for her, so we rode it over to the store room. I was not sure what she wanted to see, the room being nothing but bare adobe. She surprised me by pulling on a pair of white gloves and brushing the walls with them. She gave me an apologetic smile.

"I'm looking for dust. I shall have to come back in a few days and wipe everything with a damp cloth. I would not trust a hired servant for the job. I shall also sweep the floor, of course."

I looked down. "The floor is dry clay, and hard packed. There's not much dust."

Again the smile. "I shall trouble you for the key. We will want to be ready to move in at a moment's notice."

Somehow news of Mrs. Micarden's presence and her husband's imminent arrival had reached the ears of the *Alta California*. A few days later an item appeared on page two:

Informants tell us that an item of great importance to this city is on the way and due for arrival at any moment. Its nature remains a mystery at this time, but rumors tie it to the construction of our first lighthouse. This paper will be eager to report any new details ...

.   .   .

About ten days after Mrs. Micarden's last visit she showed up again, in early morning as before. I found her waiting at my door, looking excited judging by the way she twisted her hands together.

"The *Oriole* was sighted last night," she said. "She was hove to off the coast. The captain signaled he would wait till morning and then come in on the tide. We expect her to dock by noon."

"Excellent news," I said. "I am glad to hear Mr. Micarden and his cargo have arrived safely. I shall send a message to have my guards report for duty."

"Yes! By all means. Have your guards report to the Long Wharf at once. We shall want our goods well protected." Then she turned on her heels and was gone.

I had long since surmised that the Micarden cargo, whatever it was, was either large and heavy, or delicate, or both. If their treasure were merely gold or diamonds it would have been faster and cheaper to ship by way of the Panama route. But if someone desired to send, say a grand piano or a valuable telescope, a voyage around the Horn was the only option. An overland route of course was out of the question. I hoped the mystery of this cargo would soon be revealed.

I hurried down to the docks, after making arrangements for two guards. They appeared shortly after myself. Mrs. Micarden was already there, pacing. Also at the wharf was a Sandwich Island steamer, the *Oriental.* Mrs. Micarden ignored the fifty or so crew and passengers milling about. In due course the *Oriole* came into view around the north point. She rang her bell in greeting, and a cannon fired from land in reply.

I began to be alarmed for Mrs. Micarden. Her face was white, jaw clenched, and with perspiration on her brow. I tried to offer her a sip of brandy from my flask, but she brushed it away. This was a moment she had awaited for months. Watching her, I was not sure she would survive it.

Then the ship was docking. Her handlers made the usual fuss, with sails being hauled up and furled, hawsers tied, orders shouted. At last the gang plank clattered down. Some sailors were first off to inspect the lines, then passengers began trickling ashore, some of them struggling with luggage. A few well wishers or perhaps relatives had gathered to greet them. Finally, last of all, a gaunt tall man with wild uncut hair and beard came half stumbling down. Mrs. Micarden ran to embrace him, throwing her arms about his body at the waist. I heard her cry,

"Trefry! You are here! I knew it!"

In response I heard him murmur something like, "Of course, dear. I promised." An odd sort of greeting, I thought. It was as if his wife were not sure he would show up. I walked over and introduced myself, my two Kanakas following behind. One of them had brought a musket. Mrs. Micarden was quick to explain to her husband who I was and who they were. He listened in silence, then extended a hand and looked me in the eye. His eyes blazed. In that moment I had the impression I was greeting a madman. Then he spoke, in a mild tone.

"Please forgive my appearance, sir. I have not slept in two nights, anticipating our arrival. I trust you have made sufficient preparations for our security. We must put our equipment away as quickly as possible."

I gave the man my assurances as best I could. Mrs. Micarden continued grasping his arm as if afraid he might slip away somewhere. In due course dock wallopers unloaded the *Oriole's* cargo. Several large crates were stacked nearby on the wharf. Trefry examined them closely, looking I assumed for possible damage, and to make sure everything was there. Mrs. Micarden meanwhile had one of my guards summon a waiting teamster, who drove up with a cargo wagon pulled by four mules. Micarden himself helped load the crates. We saw them driven to my store house, unloaded and a guard posted.

Then a strange argument took place between the Micardens. It seemed Trefry wished to remain at the store room, sleeping on his crates. Hallette pleaded with him to come away to her hotel rooms, at one point tugging at his sleeve. Finally he relented and they drove off together.

That evening I described to Lisbeth what I had witnessed.

"Strange," she said, "the man hasn't seen his wife in months. It's as if his precious equipment, whatever it is, is more important to him."

Well, I thought to myself, *perhaps it is.*

I heard no more of the Micardens for more than a month, or perhaps two. In the pressure of other business I had nearly forgotten them, except for one evening at supper when Jimmy said something about "the tower." I was only half listening. "What tower is that?" I asked.

He dutifully wiped his chin before speaking. "Why, the tower on Bird Island. Alcatraz. That tower where they're going to put the lighthouse. It's going up. You can spot it from the shore. My friend Jerry Swithins owns a spy glass. He let me look. That tower will appear mighty fine when she's done."

"Well, I'm glad to hear that," I said. I wondered when Micarden would be moving his equipment out of my storehouse. It was only a few days later when Trefry paid me a visit. He got to the point.

"Are you busy sir?"

"No more than usual," I told him. "How can I serve you?"

For once his mouth spread in a smile, but I got a feeling it pained him.

"No need to serve me today, Mr. Courtenay," he said. "However, we are preparing to move our equipment to the island. My wife has told me how helpful and cooperative you have been. I thought perhaps you might like to see what we have been guarding so carefully."

"By all means," I said. I put my coat on and joined him at his buggy. It was but a short drive to the storehouse. On the way I had a chance to observe the man at close range. I had the impression he was somehow frail and incapable of any physical exertion. I thought I noted a faint sour smell from him that did not come from poor hygiene. In fact his clothing and body appeared spotless, face drawn and pale. He looked like a man who had gone without sleep, working long and hard for many days.

"Here we are," he said, halting at the store room. The door was standing open, one of my guards to one side. We dismounted and entered, to find Mrs. Micarden standing aside as if awaiting us. She said, not glancing at me,

"Dear, you must eat something. This soup is still warm."

"In a minute, dear. I just want to show Mr. Courtenay what we have." He stood next to a large brass object with a familiar shape, but much larger than any I had ever seen before. "This is the Argand lamp," he explained. "It will burn whale oil, which should work quite well. It's practically smokeless. This particular lamp was made in France, to our requirements."

I spent a moment admiring the lamp, which was indeed a fine piece of workmanship. Micarden moved to another object, this one more incomprehensible, with chains, gears, and lead weights. Mrs. Micarden in the meantime had somehow pushed a bowl of soup into her husband's hands. He spooned some into his mouth and put the bowl down again, as if paying no attention to it.

"This device is the clockwork," he said. "It may not look like much, but once installed it will rotate the lens for two hours before rewinding. The keeper need only pull on the weight to keep our machine running."

I nodded, unable to think of an intelligent comment. The device made me think of a dismantled grandfather clock.

"And finally," Micarden said, "We have here the eye of the lighthouse." He stood by a large object completely covered with white linen. I had no idea what it might be. "You could say," Micarden went on, "the lamp or its oil is the lighthouse's food. The clockwork is both muscle and brain. This is its heart and eye." With that, he whipped off its linen cover.

I stood for a moment, blinking and baffled. I had never seen the like. The object was in several parts, not connected. It was made of glass, but not in any form I could understand. I looked at Micarden and merely shrugged. With that he grinned.

"It's a third order Fresnel lens," he said. "I won't tell you what it cost, but it's worth a fortune. Do you wonder it's under guard? I say, it took some doing to get the Lighthouse Board to go for the investment. When it's fully assembled in place, it will put a light fifteen miles or so out to sea." He took a step back, silently inspecting his wonderful lens. He drew a cloth from a pocket and brushed away a speck of dust, then said in a low tone, "It's beautiful, isn't it?"

A ray of sunlight struck a corner of glass and dazzled me. "Yes," I said. "It is beautiful."

A few days later Mrs. Micarden appeared again at my warehouse, this time in the afternoon. I offered her coffee.

"Lisbeth had quite a time teaching me to brew coffee," I told her. "It's quite passable, at least if you add sugar."

She smiled. "Thank you, but no sir. I wish only to settle our bill. All of our equipment has been transferred to the island. I thanked your guards for their service and paid them some extra remuneration. We shan't need them on Alcatraz, since the only other people there are soldiers."

"Well, it has been a pleasure serving you, madam. I hope we shall see more of you and Mr. Micarden." I drew a ledger from my desk and made out a bill. The amount still owed was not large.

"Mrs. Courtenay has been kind enough to invite me for supper tomorrow," she said. "I'm afraid my husband will be spending most of his time henceforth at the island. There are no accommodations as yet for ladies."

Indeed she did appear the next evening at our supper table. Jimmy stared at her open-mouthed, as if awestruck. Mrs. Micarden asked us all to call her Hallette, and spent some time praising Lisbeth's kitchen artistry. Half way through the meal she turned to Jimmy and asked him what he was planning to do when he got older.

"I want to build stuff," he replied. "Like lighthouses and bridges and things."

"Ah. A fine ambition. You shall have to go to school for that."

"I go to school two days a week. I'm learnin' how to read and figure."

I gave him a nod. "And doing well at it, I hear. As yet there are not many books to read, but I hope to be getting more soon."

Lisbeth turned to Hallette. "Mr. Micarden is an engineer, I guess."

"Yes. He went to Harvard. First in his class." For a moment her expression was one of sadness, but then a smile broke through as she turned back to Jimmy. "I shall bring you a book. It's an illustrated history of lighthouses."

M rs. Micarden and Lisbeth continued to visit at least once a week. Several times she was over for supper, but I gathered she kept busy traveling to Alcatraz and back, visiting her husband and seeing he was provided for. In fact, months passed. The shipment from the *Oriole* had arrived in October. Construction on the island was delayed during the winter due to problems of delivering supplies such as lumber. Mr. Micarden remained on Alcatraz. Finally, in late May, Lisbeth announced to me that both Mr. and Mrs. Micarden would be coming for Sunday supper after church. Accordingly, I wore my best suit in which to receive them.

When they appeared that afternoon, I was appalled at Trevry Micarden's appearance. The last time I had seen him I thought him ill. Now he looked gaunt and haggard, a man nearly at the end of his rope. I of course pretended not to notice.

Then Jimmy spoke up and asked Mr. Micarden if he would build more lighthouses when he had finished the first. Trefry gave the boy a weak smile.

"Perhaps I shall. There are more to be built, you know. However, I think I may have to leave California for awhile, because of the press of other business."

Before the boy could attempt to pry further, Lisbeth said, "It must give great satisfaction to know you have created the first lighthouse on the Coast."

"Indeed." Trefry looked at his wife, then at each of us in turn. He nodded. "A light will shine upon the waters. A light will shine for years to come."

Before supper was over, he had an announcement to make. "Hallette will be joining me on Alcatraz tomorrow. The house is completed, so we shall be staying there for a few days, until the regular keepers arrive. All of our equipment is installed and ready to be tested. I still need to make some final delicate adjustments to the Fresnel lens." He gave us each a look from across the table.

"I feel rather like a diamond cutter making the final polish on a rare gem. Except, of course, that it's so much larger."

Lisbeth smiled. "And so much more beautiful, I expect." Micarden looked pleased.

After a moment's pause I said, "I assume you will be returning to the city when you are done?"

He turned to look at his wife, who looked straight ahead. "At least Hallette will," he said.

San Francisco is often cold and foggy in the summer months, but this June began as a beautiful promise. The air was clear and blue, sea calm, sunshine warm. I went about my business, nearly forgetting the Micardens. I let it be known at the Wharf that my extra store room was empty and for rent. Then, shortly after sundown on Thursday, June First, Jimmy came bursting into our house.

"Come and see!" he shouted.

"See what, Jimmy?" I got to my feet at once, expecting some disaster, perhaps another great fire in the city.

"Come on and look!" He was jumping up and down. I put aside my pipe and the *AltaCalifornia* and followed him outside. He grabbed my coat sleeve and pulled me in the direction of a nearby sand hill. "Come on, Mr. Courtenay! You can see from up there!"

Jimmy ran to the top of the hill and I struggled after him. The sky was not yet quite dark, or I probably would have stumbled. We reached the top. Jimmy pointed into the darkness of the east. For a moment I could see nothing. Then a diamond-brilliant light flashed.

"It's the lighthouse," he nearly screamed. "On Alcatraz! It's our first lighthouse!"

I didn't know what to say. We both watched in silence for several minutes, watched the beam sweep around and flash in its regular measured intervals. Finally I said, "That's surely something, Jimmy. That's something."

The sky above grew darker. We went back down the hill.

Next day, the *Alta* carried a brief notice about the first appearance of the light. I found no mention of Trefry Micarden. Later I learned that the account was inaccurate: it gave the height of the tower as 160 feet above water level, whereas it was actually only half that. For about a week I heard nothing more about the light or the Micardens. The beam came alive each sunset; now and then I climbed the hill again or went elsewhere for a view of the bay. The light continued to shine.

Then, on a Saturday after work, I came home to find Mrs. Micarden in our parlor, sitting with Lisbeth. Jimmy was nowhere to be seen; I expected Lisbeth had sent him on some errand to get him out of the way. From Hallette's reddened eyes I guessed she had been weeping. I realized she was dressed in black, unlike her usual bright colors.

Lisbeth gave me a desperate look. We have known each other long enough to understand the meaning of each look. This one meant, among other things, *Be careful what you say*. And also, *Please help*. But of course I did not know what was wrong. Mrs. Micarden gave me a glance, then turned back to Lisbeth and simply stared, as if awaiting an answer to some question asked before I entered.

Feeling awkward, I noticed that Lisbeth had served coffee. I poured myself a cup and then sat in my usual chair. Finally I cleared my throat and said, "Will Mr. Micarden be joining us?"

Hallette turned to me, her eyes without expression. She said, "I will be joining him tomorrow. I have arranged for burial at sea, as he wished. I have chartered a boat."

At this I nearly dropped my coffee cup. I arose and sputtered something, I'm not sure what.

Mrs. Micarden said, "Trefry died, at last, yesterday. We had already made all necessary preparations. As soon as our business is finished I shall return to New York. I came over merely to thank you both for your kindness, and to say goodbye."

Lisbeth cleared her throat and said in a low tone, "Mr. Micarden, it seems, had been ill for some time."

Hallette nodded. "Yes, he was. Oh, but of course you had no way of knowing. The doctors told us before we left the east. They said he could not survive the voyage to California." She began to weep again but did not attempt to dry her eyes, as if unaware of her own tears.

"Everyone expected him to leave the Lighthouse Board and turn the project over to someone else, but he would have none of it. The directors learned somehow of his illness and attempted to dismiss him, but they had already signed a contract they were unable or unwilling to break. When I said farewell to Trefry I expected not to see him again. I wanted to sail with him but he insisted I go ahead to prepare. He always believed he would get here alive. He said, *I shall not leave you before our light shines.* That's what he told me." Here she stopped speaking for several minutes, with silent sobs. Lisbeth reached out and took her hand but said nothing.

Finally Hallette's weeping faded and ceased. She dried her tears and took a sip of coffee. She said, "It was the lens that kept him alive. I would like to think it was my love that did it, but I have not that power. He refused to die until his lens was installed and shining." At that she fell silent.

It was then I realized that Trefry Micarden was mad. Only a madman, a maniac, could have the will to defy death for the sake of a lens, a great light. I was sure that he loved Hallette, but that love was less than his mania, his obsession. I gave a silent prayer for the peace of his soul.

That was the last time I saw Hallette Micarden. There was no memorial service, not even an obituary. It was as if the couple had never been to this city. A few days later a steamer left for Panama, and I learned that Hallette's name was on the passenger list. On Sunday evening I brought Lisbeth and Jimmy down to the wharf at sunset so that they could see the light.

"Burial at sea," Lisbeth said. "It's so sad, not having so much as a monument."

I turned to her in surprise. "You can't be serious," I said. I pointed at the Alcatraz light. "We are all flashes of light in this vast darkness. Have you ever seen a finer monument?"

The End

THE CASE OF MARTEN OMAN

7

SAN FRANCISCO, 1856

Deposition of Hyram R. Courtenay
before the tribunal of the second Committee of Vigilance

M y name is Hyram L. Courtenay. I don't usually use my middle
name because I don't much like it. My profession is warehouseman. I have resided in this city since the year 1847 together with my wife
Lisbeth. My address is Rincon Hill. I first met Mr. Marten Oman at the
Mechanic's Institute ...

T he prosecuting attorney, Mr. Lehman, dropped his hand,
holding the deposition at his side. He said, "Is the testimony in
this document yours, sir, and is it accurate?"

I gave him a sidelong look before responding. I wanted him to
think I was mulling over his question. I just wanted to slow him down
a bit. I said, "Yes sir, to the best of my knowledge, that is an accurate
account."

Lehman rubbed his beard a moment before glancing around the

"courtroom." Actually, it was a room in back of Sam Brannan's store. It wasn't a big crowd; only three men instead of a regular jury, about a dozen spectators. I saw four women in back, Belle Cora's ladies. She herself had been asked not to come. Sitting at a table to one side was the defendant, Marten Oman, with bowed head. His attorney, Edward McGowan, sat next to him. I don't believe Lehman was an actual lawyer, but McGowan used to be a judge.

Lehman turned back to me. "Now, Mr. Courtenay. Let's try to keep this procedure a little less formal. As you are aware, the defendant, Mr. Oman, was arrested by the Committee of Vigilance because our local constables considered this affair beneath notice. I would like to know how you, Mr. Courtenay, feel about the Committee of Vigilance and our procedures here?"

I cleared my throat and took a sip of water before speaking. I said, "Mr. Lehman, as you well know, I have never been a member of the Committee, which I hear now numbers about six thousand. I have at times spoken out against some activities of this Committee. However, I recognize your good intentions. Lacking an effective justice system, as we do in this city, I can see how—"

He cut me off. "Yes, yes. We all know your views in the matter. I really mean to ask about your feeling in this particular case? Are you for or against the defendant?"

At this I answered at once, looking him in the eye. "Neither, sir. I make no judgments. I only testify to the facts as I know them. Judgment is the job of God and of this tribunal."

"Ah. Yes, a good answer, sir. Perhaps, then, you might simply tell us what you know, with no further questions from myself."

"Very well, sir. As I said in my deposition, I first met Mr. Oman at the Mechanic's Institute."

~

I had always considered the Institute a refuge from the chaos which usually envelops the rest of the city. Already this year we have witnessed hundreds of homicides and not a few lynchings perpetrated by those not of this Committee. Let me say that I am impressed by the great restraint shown by this Committee of Vigilance, in hanging only a small number of those arrested.

But, to the point. I had repaired to the Institute to enjoy two or three hours of quiet study and contemplation in the library. This place has always been a refuge from disorder and barbarism; by unspoken rule one speaks in low tones so as not to disturb other readers. Today however proved an exception; I had been perusing a world atlas when a loud voice disturbed my concentration. I looked up to discover an unkempt and unruly person had somehow blundered in. His dress was ragged and dirty, his beard and hair unkempt. And I might say, he seemed about the size of a small ox.

"*Where's the bar?*" he shouted. And, "I need a drink! Show me to your damn *bar!*"

For a moment I was at a loss how to act. I began to rise from my table, but then a young man stepped forward from behind a row of shelves. This man was large, but smaller than the ox. He was clean shaven, dressed in neat working man's clothing, and with blonde hair.

He said in a mild tone, "There is no bar here, sir. You are in the wrong place and making too much noise. You will have to leave."

"*Says you!*" the larger man shouted. "I said I want a drink, and I'll damn well have one!" At this point he drew forth a large Bowie knife and began waving it. I recall wondering for a moment how sharp it might be; it might have been as unkempt as its owner.

By this time I had risen to my feet. Having no weapon of my own I lifted the heavy atlas, preparing to throw it. However, the young man with yellow hair simply moved in front of the ox, ignoring the knife. He said not a word, but I saw his arm shoot forward and connect with the large man's jaw. The bigger man dropped like a stone.

My own jaw fell open. I had never witnessed such a feat. I have watched a number of boxing matches and never seen a man rendered unconscious with a single blow, especially not a person of this size. The knife clattered to the floor, and the younger man kicked it away. I came forward, still holding the atlas just in case.

I said, "That was remarkable, sir. I have never seen such pugilisim in my life."

"I did my share of boxing in the navy," he said. He gave a short bow and extended a hand. "Marten Oman at your service."

"Hyram Courtenay." I glanced at the body on the floor. The man had groaned, which meant he was still among the living. "We had best get this out of here before it comes to."

Marten grinned and nodded. Together we heaved on the man's legs, dragged him downstairs and left him in the alley.

"Now perhaps," I said, "you might do me the honor of repairing to that saloon across the street for a cool pint."

He favored me with a broad grin. "Don't mind if I do, sir."

That was how we met, and how we quickly became fast friends. It turned out that Mr. Oman was an avid player of chess, something not easy to find in this city. We agreed to meet at the Institute a few days later for a serious match. Soon we had evolved a habit of meeting once a week for the same purpose. As you can see, Mr. Oman is about half my age. Such friendships are perhaps unusual.

He was not verbose about his own background, and in fact for the most part had few comments about the world. However, I did manage to draw him out since he was not reluctant to answer questions.

"I'm really a Swede," he told me on our second or third meeting. "That is, I was born in a village on the coast of Sweden, but my parents emigrated while I was young. At the age of twelve I seized the opportunity to enlist in the American navy as powder monkey. My parents were quite poor and had no objection, since by then they had three other mouths to feed, two of my brothers and a sister. No, sir, I know not what has become of my family, whether they lived or died. Since coming to shore I have sent off many letters, none of them answered." Here Marten gave a shrug.

"Such is life. Perhaps one day I shall know more. In the meantime, I remember them in my prayers."

I mention these details, gentlemen, to impress upon you that Mr. Oman is a gentleman at heart, a loving son and brother, and not a criminal. He is as well a veteran of our navy, and was at Vera Cruz in the Mexican War.

Now, when first we met Mr. Oman was working at some sort of job down at the waterfront. I was never clear on exactly what he did there, though I know it had something to do with overhauling ships and boats. Then one day he appeared for our usual appointment wearing a new suit and looking prosperous. I could not help commenting on his improved appearance.

"Ah," he said, "thank you, sir. I'm not used to fashion, but I hope I make a good impression. If you say this is okay, then I guess I'm set."

Although curious, I posed no questions. I always assume a man will tell me what I need to know. After we had set up our chess board and chosen sides, he said,

"I have taken on a new job, you see. I'm no longer at the waterfront."

I still made no comment, merely nodded to show I heard. A few minutes later, after losing two pawns, he said, "I am now employed by Madame Belle Cora."

At this I could not help being startled. I sat back and stared at him for a moment. Marten grinned and also sat back, with a satisfied smile.

"Oh, I know what you're thinking, sir. But I don't feel I'm doing anything improper. Belle Cora runs the finest parlor house in San Francisco, and many of the city's finest gentlemen visit there. After the recent death of her husband she needed a business manager, and sometimes bouncer. My duties are mainly seeing bills are paid to vendors, and making sure no one steals supplies. And also, occasionally, ejecting an unruly customer. But that doesn't happen often, her home being first class."

I had to clear my throat. "You are aware, I assume, that her husband was recently hanged by the Committee of Vigilance."

At this he looked sad. "Yes, so I understand. Madam Cora believes he didn't deserve it. She says it was self defense, or accidental. As to that, I wouldn't know."

He offered nothing more, so after a minute or so of moving pieces on our board, I asked, "Tell me, Marten. How did you come into this position of employment?"

He shrugged, looking away from the table. "I answered a notice in the *Alta California*. Mrs. Cora interviewed half a dozen applicants and chose me because I was qualified. I was able to gain an education while in the navy, you see. I'm quite good at keeping books. So can Mrs. Cora, as far as that goes, but I can relieve her of that burden."

I commented that while I had never entered that establishment, being happily married and a church goer, I had heard it was the finest house in San Francisco. At this he laughed.

"A great many of Madam Cora's clientele are happily married church goers. But yes, it is truly a fine place. The curtains are white lace and crimson damask. She has the finest possible furniture. If you like, I can see you get an invitation to the next soiree. Some of our most prominent citizens will attend, judges and aldermen and such."

I thanked him, but declined. I didn't think Lisbeth would approve, and I could never keep a secret from her.

We continued meeting once a week or so, sometimes twice. Marten seemed contented and happy with his chosen career. Once he told me,

"Oh, I know it's not considered respectable. If I were to find my parents or family I wouldn't be able to tell them where I work. I would be disgraced. But then, they will probably never know, if they're still alive." He paused a moment, thinking, then added, "Mrs. Belle Cora is one of the finest ladies I have met. She is honorable and brave. Never mind her profession, she's no worse than the judges and policemen and preachers who frequent her establishment. She stood up for her husband while he lived. No one could have done more for him."

Now, please do not take offense, gentlemen, but Marten also mentioned that he had seen a number of members of this Vigilance Committee at Mrs. Cora's house. He could have mentioned names to me, but declined to do so out of a sense of honor.

Then one day Mr. Oman showed up at the Mechanic's Institute looking somewhat drawn and haggard. His face was pale and he was unshaved, his neck tie unknotted. We sat down to the chess board, but he seemed unable to concentrate. Finally I asked him if something was wrong. He gave me a strange look.

"Mrs. Cora was terribly angry this morning. I have never seen her in such a state. I was afraid she might do something violent."

I moved a rook on the board. "What about?"

He pulled a crumpled paper from a pocket inside his coat. "About this. Have you ever looked at this rag?"

It was a copy of *The Bugle*. I am sure you are all familiar with this scandal sheet, since it's hawked on nearly every street corner. I told Marten that I had seen it before, but had no interest in reading it. He waved it in front of my face.

"This is the worst garbage ever printed! It's nothing but lies, libel and baseless rumors."

I had to agree. "Mr. Isaac Welch is the editor. I've never met him, and don't know anyone who has. I suspect he goes out in disguise so that no one will assassinate him. Most of *The Bugle* is devoted to attacks on bordellos and parlor houses, as well as on their proprietors. It amounts to free advertising for the whore houses."

Marten nodded, opened the paper to its second page, and began to read. "It seems Madame C. of recent Vigilante fame, although still wearing her widow's weeds, has taken on a personal fancy boy, a handsome and brawny fellow. If all his parts are as large as the rest of him, the good Madame must be well satisfied."

Marten crumpled the paper and tore it to bits. "There's more, but I won't read it to you. It's obscene. It's dishonorable and disgusting."

"I'm sorry you came to Welch's notice," I said. "But then again, Welch hates everybody, so why should you be an exception?"

"Pah!" Marten swept up all the chess pieces with one hand and dumped them into their storage box. "I'm not concerned about my own reputation. It's the libel against Belle that riles me. She is a lady of the first quality and does not deserve such vileness."

"Has she seen the paper?"

"Of course. She reads every issue, as do all the bordello madams. They feel left out if Welch doesn't attack them. And men read the paper to find out if there are any new women in town. A disgusting business, but there it is."

"Mrs. Cora was upset, I take it?"

He shook his head. "She was, but no more than myself. If I find Welch I mean to wring his neck."

I told Marten I hoped he would restrain himself. He looked thoughtful a moment, then said,

"If Welch has no informer placed in the house, then he must have visited there himself. He might even be one of the regular customers."

"Please do not kill him," I said. But of course that was exactly what he did.

Not right away, of course. I saw Marten a few days later when he dropped in to my warehouse where I was working. He had what I would call a satisfied expression.

"I found Mr. Welch," he said.

I paused at whatever I was doing at the time. "Ah," I said. "You spoke to him, then?"

"No. I just wanted to find out who he is. It wasn't that hard. The name of his printer is on the first page of every copy of *The Bugle*. I interviewed the gentleman who runs the print shop. I asked him Welch's address. I made up some story about my owing him money. The man told me he didn't know where Welch lives. Seems he's in the habit of changing rooms about once a month. But he did tell me he would be coming in on Friday afternoon to pick up next week's edition.

"So I simply took a discrete position across the street on Friday, and waited. Sure enough he showed up with a wagon just before closing time. I got to see what he looks like. Then I understood how he knows so much about what goes on at Mrs. Cora's house, as well as the other establishments. There is no spy in our midst. Mr. Welch is a regular customer of ours, under a different name."

I nodded. "That would make sense. It would also mean that our Mr. Welch is an unbounded hypocrite."

"Indeed. I just haven't decided yet what to do about him. We could simply ban him from entering the house again, but that would not stop his lies and slanders. Or I could publicly expose him, but I'm not sure that would stop him either."

I said, "Perhaps the best thing to do would be nothing. He's bound to get tired of harassing Madam Cora and turn his attention elsewhere. Why give the man more fuel for his hate?"

Marten gazed into space a moment. "Perhaps you are right, sir. I will have to think the matter over. At least I know now how Welch got the names of all Mrs. Cora's girls, and how he learned about me. I will take your advice under consideration. Thank you."

And with that he turned and left. I hoped this would be the end of the affair, but of course it was not. Mr. Oman did not show up for our regular chess play that week. I was a bit concerned, but not greatly worried; I calculated that Mrs. Cora had probably given him other business to attend to. Then, a day or two later I was on my way to the warehouse when I heard a newsboy hawking the morning headlines: *Editor Assassinated,* or some such phrase. I immediately halted my buggy and purchased a *Morning Call.* I learned that our Mr. Welch had been found dead in the street, of a broken neck. I was of course horrified. I immediately thought of *The Bulletin's* previous editor, for whose murder Mrs. Cora's husband was hanged.

The *Call* claimed there were no suspects, and that no witnesses had yet come forward. Perhaps I should have come forward myself, to voice my fears to the Sheriff, but then I did not wish to jump to conclusions. Welch could have been attacked by nearly anyone. I decided to say nothing until I could speak to Mr. Oman.

As it turned out, Marten showed up at my door the following morning. He had never been to my home before—Lisbeth would not have approved—but of course everyone knows where I live. Instead of going to my warehouse, we went to a nearby coffee house. We sat down at a table, neither of us having spoken more than two words. Finally Marten looked up at me and said, "I did it."

I took a deep breath. Then I said, "You did what, Marten?"

"I killed Isaac Welch. He made me extremely angry. He threatened Mrs. Cora. He began shaking his fist in my face, and I lost my

temper. I'm not quite sure what happened, but I must have struck
him. Next thing I knew he was on the ground. I tried to get him up
again, but he was dead. I shall turn myself in now. Will you go
with me?"

"Of course," I said. "But perhaps you should eat something first.
You look terrible, your shirt is torn. Have you been back to Mrs.
Cora's?"

"No, sir, I couldn't. I slept in a horse barn last night."

And that, gentlemen, is the end of my testimony. I made Marten
eat some eggs and bacon, and went to the Sheriff's office where he
surrendered. That very evening members of your Vigilance
Committee demanded the Sheriff turn him over. Since the
Committee is better armed than the Sheriff he had no choice but to
comply. And so Marten sits before this tribunal, who shall decide his
fate. I hope, gentlemen, that you will find it in your hearts to show
him mercy.

$\sim$

At this point there was a brief adjournment, of half an hour or
so. Marten was led away in shackles and I had no chance to
speak to him. When his trial resumed, Marten's appointed counsel,
Edward McGowan,came forward. I learned later that he had been
one of Mrs. Cora's favorite clients.

"Gentlemen of the Tribunal," he said, in an oratorical tone, "the
defendant, Marten Oman, wishes to make a statement in his
defense."

The tribunal readily agreed, and Marten came forward. He had
cleaned up some, but still looked worn and pale. This is what he said
to the court, as nearly as I can recall his words:

"It is true, gentlemen, that I killed Isaac Welch. I understand that
your verdict will depend in part on your determination as to
whether my crime was premeditated. I can only state that I had no

intention to kill Mr. Welch when I went to meet him. I will however admit that I had previously considered the idea. But I am not a murderer by nature. I meant only to confront the man.

"What occasioned our meeting was a letter delivered to Mrs. Cora's house the previous day. As you know, since Mr. Cora's death I have been engaged to handle some of Mrs. Cora's business affairs. Part of my duties is to screen her mail, separating personal messages from commercial. In this case I could not tell from the envelope which it was, since I saw no return address. I therefore opened it, and found myself horrified.

"The missive was from Mr. Welch. You may read it yourself, since I have entrusted it to my council, Mr. McGowan. Simply stated, it was an attempt at extortion. Mr. Welch wished to blackmail Belle Cora. He demanded ten thousand dollars in cash, to be delivered at once. He did allow that if she was unable to raise that much on short notice he would accept a partial payment to show 'good faith.'

"If Mrs. Cora refused to comply, Welch intended to publish a complete list of her more respectable clients. Included with the letter was such a list. I recognized many of the names. They include men well known to high society: judges, lawyers, doctors, aldermen, capitalists. I dare say the list includes some members of this Committee. Naturally, if made public this list would ruin Mrs. Cora since she would lose all future clients.

"Welch's letter demanded that Mrs. Cora either appear herself or send a reliable messenger to meet Mr. Welch. He specified a certain public street corner. I imagine he considered he would be safer negotiating in public rather than in private rooms. As it turned out, he was mistaken.

"At no time did I show the letter to Mrs. Cora. Even now she is unaware of its existence. I determined I would meet Welch myself. I am not sure what my plan was, except confrontation. I certainly would not offer him money. I hoped to convince him that were he to publish the list he would be subject to lawsuit. When I met the man I did threaten him with Law, but he merely laughed. He said he is sued two or three times a month. The more suits, the more papers sold.

"Isaac Welch was the worst man I have ever met. The more I threatened, the more he sneered and laughed. At one point he promised to publish the first ten names on his list in the next edition of *The Bugle*. Unless Mrs. Cora complied, the next ten would come out the following week, and so on. There are two hundred names on that list, gentlemen.

"Finally, Mr. Welch began to threaten violence. He began to curse and to call me obscene names. I could see him working himself up, until he was shouting with a red face, and drooling. Then he began driving a finger into my chest, as hard as he could. That was when I lost my temper and struck the man. I hit him only once. I understand the coroner has determined that his neck was broken by the force of my blow.

"I know I was wrong to leave the scene, but I was badly shaken. I hardly realized what had occurred. Mr. Welch lay on the ground without moving. I think I had some idea of going for help, but found myself trembling badly. I found a saloon and had a drink. Then I wandered about for some time, until going to see Mr. Courtenay the following day.

"That is all of my statement, gentlemen. I make no excuses. It is for you to judge my guilt or innocence. Thank you."

Without waiting for questions, Marten turned and sat down. Mr. McGowan arose and addressed the tribunal.

"Gentlemen, you have heard a statement from the defendant. As you know, Mrs. Belle Cora has no love for the Committee of Vigilance. It might be fair to say she hates us. I can only ask that you do not take Mrs. Cora's feelings into account when arriving at a verdict. This young man had nothing to do with her previous disputes, or with her husband, whom he never met. Now, I present in evidence the letter and list which Mr. Oman has described."

With that, he withdrew a fat envelope from an inner pocket and handed it over to the tribunal. It was accepted, and the court adjourned to await a verdict.

◊

"And so," I said to my listener, "That is my complete account of the case of Marten Oman. I was not present during the verdict or sentencing, having been asked to leave the court room. This trial was held in secret, and nothing ever published. You say you are writing a book about the Vigilantes. I wish you luck, sir. You have only my word for what went on that day. I can't say if anyone will believe you or not."

"Well, what was the verdict?" my interviewer asked. "And the sentence, if any?"

At that I had to light my pipe and take a puff or two, remembering. Finally I said, "The verdict was death, sir."

"Ah. Then they hanged Mr. Oman."

I studied my visitor, trying to see if he might understand. With all my years in San Francisco, there are still things about this city I do not. "No sir," I said. "The Committee decided to let Marten go. I guess it was that list of Mrs. Cora's customers that decided them. They called it justifiable homicide. The last I heard of Mr. Oman, he re-enlisted in the navy as a lieutenant. I don't know what has become of him since."

My visitor shook his head in bewilderment. "But then, why did you just tell me the verdict was death?"

I studied the bowl of my pipe. A good smoke can be a great comfort. "Oh, as to that," I said. "This was not a regular court of law, you understand, this was the Committee of Vigilance, with their own rules, which they sometimes made up as they went. Yes, there was a sentence of death. But it was not against Marten Oman.

"It was passed on Isaac Welch. Posthumously. Please have another sip of brandy, sir. You look dry."

THE NUGGET

8

SAN FRANCISCO, 1852

I guess you want another story about the gold rush. You newspaper folks are all alike. You get paid for writing down other people's yarns when you get tired of making up your own. Well, I don't really mind because I enjoy telling tales. Just don't accuse me of lying. Maybe I am and maybe I'm not.

My lady Lisbeth and myself, we have lived here in San Francisco since it was Yerba Buena. I must say we each could spin off some strange and marvelous yarns about things we have seen and heard. Some you would believe and some you'd scoff at. Me, I don't care, long as I get to tell them. What comes to mind today was a fellow I met once or twice, name of Edwyn Fohler. German immigrant, he was. You must have noticed we have a lot of immigrants in this town, German, French, Chilean, Australian, Chinese, you name it. I met Mr. Fohler one day down at Sam Brannan's dry goods store where I went to see about a delivery. Brannan was getting rich selling picks and shovels to the miners, most of whom stayed broke. A lot of his goods I kept in my warehouse until he had room for them. Anyway, Mr. Fohler approached me while I was waiting for Brannan to deal with another customer.

"Sir," he said to me, "I can see by your dress and demeanor you are a respectable business man. Perhaps you might advise me." His English was about perfect, though with a slight accent. He was a short fellow with round eyeglasses. I would have taken him for a store clerk.

"Don't know about respectable," I said, "but I'm in business. How I could I help a fellow like yourself?"

He gave a big smile, like someone who had just won a jackpot. "My name is Mister EdwynFohler," he said. "I am off to the mines. Just as soon as I am able to equip myself."

"Congratulations," I told him. I gave him my own name, Hyram Courtenay. I thought of warning him not to let Brannan take all his money, but thought better of it, Brannan being a friend and all. "What can I do for you, sir?"

He rubbed his hands together. I noticed they were not the sort of hands that looked as if they had ever held a pick and shovel.

"I will be in need of a partner," he said. "Perhaps two or three. I have thought about forming a mining company. I hoped perhaps you might steer me toward some reputable and honest men who might be interested."

At that I asked Herr Fohler how long he had been in California.

"Three days. I came aboard the *Californian*. Why do you ask, sir?"

I couldn't help grinning. "Just that when you have been in San Francisco for awhile you will come to recognize that it's not an easy thing to find one reputable and honest man. Myself excepted, of course. But you shouldn't have any trouble finding a partner once you get to the gold fields. You need more than one to work a claim."

"I see." He looked thoughtful. "Well sir, I do come prepared. I have studied geology and modern mining methods, having read several books on the subject. I understand panning and sluicing and hydraulics. But I am not what you would call experienced, as such."

"Go on up to the fields then," I told him. "Far be it for me to discourage a man. You'll get the experience soon enough. Ah, but excuse me; I see Mr. Brannan wants me."

I took care of my own business quickly enough and left Herr Fohler in the store, to the mercies of Sam Brannan. I didn't expect I was likely to see Fohler again. He was one among thousands headed for the hills, to find either riches or frustration. On my way out I wished him well; he smiled and waved. I do not know if he ever smiled again after that day.

By coincidence, I did catch a glimpse of him once before he left town. I went to the docks to meet the ferry from Sacramento because a business partner was due back from a brief trip. After passengers had debarked and cargo was unloading, a group of men pushed forward preparing to board. I was surprised to notice Fohler among them. He saw me in turn and paused a moment.

"Good morning, sir!" He gave a quick bow. "I wish to thank you for your advice and hospitality of the other day. I have indeed found a partner to accompany me to the mines. This is Hans. I'm afraid he speaks no English; please forgive him."

The man next to him stepped forward after Fohler spoke a few words in German. He bowed in turn and extended a hand, which I took. I had a moment of fear that he might squeeze too hard; his hand was twice the size of mine, and sinewy. The man himself was equally huge, broad in both shoulders and jaw. In fact I judged him twice the mass of Herr Fohler. I guessed he would do well in shoveling dirt, if nothing else.

"And now please excuse us." Fohler gave another quick bow. "We must board the ferry. We are off to gain our fortunes!" And they both hurried on to the boat.

I thought no more of Herr Fohler or his massive partner. Indeed, when four or five months had passed I had forgotten all about them. There were many other people and things to capture my attention here. Then, on a Sunday afternoon when Lisbeth and I returned from church, a messenger came to my door bearing an odd note. It said,

. . .

Mr. Courtenay,
        I hope you will have the kindness and time to pay me a brief visit at City Hospital. I fear I am in a bad way. You are one of the few men in this city whose name I know. There is something of which I must unburden myself before I am too late. P.S. I asked Mr. Brannan to come, but he says he has not the time.
    Yours sincerely,
    Edwyn Fohler

I showed the note to Lisbeth and asked what she thought of it. She merely shrugged and told me to go and see what the man wanted. She promised to hold my supper.

And so I hitched up our trap and drove down to the hospital. I confess this institution is not always well regarded, but I think they try their best. Anyone who can not pay is treated free. I found Fohler in a room by himself. There were two other beds, but they were empty at least for now. The place looked clean enough, but hardly what I would call luxury.

"It is so good of you to come. I had feared myself abandoned by humanity." He waved at the rest of the room. "I had enough gold left to pay for this, but little else. Ah, but fear not. I asked you to come not to beg for money. I wish to make my confession."

An odd remark, I thought. Perhaps the man was not quite right in the head. Indeed he had changed since last I saw him. His cheeks were sunken, eyes hollow, and his hands trembled. I noticed he had lost a few teeth, which I thought might have been due to a bout with scurvy.

"Possibly you have me confused with someone else," I said. "I am not your priest or confessor."

"Pah!" He waved a hand as if brushing a fly. "As to that, a priest has already been. I told him all, but it did me no good. He is sworn to secrecy. I must unburden myself to someone who will not stop at spreading knowledge of my sins far and wide. My only salvation is to make my evil known and public." He gestured once more at the room. "They tell me I have brain fever. If by some chance I should survive this, which I believe unlikely, I intend to depose myself before your sheriff or constable. I deserve to hang."

He interrupted himself with a fit of coughing. I fetched him a glass of water which he sipped and then downed in a few swallows.

"But first," he said, "if you will look to that small cabinet by my bed. Please open the drawer."

I did as he bid and removed a thick envelope. There was an address in German written on the front.

"A letter to my brother," Fohler said. "I pray that you may help me by seeing it posted. I am happy to pay you for the fee and for any trouble."

"I shall see it posted tomorrow morning. Never mind the fee. Is there aught else I might help you with?"

"No, only by listening. Oh well, one other thing perhaps, but I shall tell you when I finish. I would have asked the doctor to post my letter, but frankly I do not quite trust him not to throw it away. There are so few men here I feel I can trust. Truth to tell, I am not even sure of your Sam Brannan."

I nearly laughed at that, thinking of a few others who might have made the same claim. But before I could respond, I realized that Fohler had already launched into his confession.

"At first," he said, "Hans and I got along famously. As it turned out we were both from the same province in Bavaria, and so had much in common. We suspected we might even be distant relatives. After leaving this city we went to Sonora and soon found ourselves working on the Stanislaus River.

"When I say working, I do not exaggerate. I soon discovered that working a gold claim in reality bears little resemblance to what I had read in the manuals of geology. I sold the wagon and horse for money to live on. Then we spent our last cash to buy a claim from three men who wanted to leave. Hans and I found ourselves laboring from dawn to dusk on the river bank, digging and sluicing gravel. By the second or third day my hands were covered with blisters, and my back was the purest pain.

"Hans fared somewhat better, being more accustomed to manual labor. But even he soon began to be poorly. Our diet was mainly beans, coffee and sourdough bread. The weather was bitter cold, and it seemed our clothing was always damp. By the third month Hans had developed a persistent cough, and I feared consumption. We ate what meat we could shoot or catch, such as squirrels or birds.

"However, we stayed by our claim. After all, we were taking out a few ounces of color each day. We put our gold dust in sacks and hid them away. Toward the end, I weighed our treasure and realized we had earned just enough to repay my initial investment in wagon and supplies. To say I felt disappointment would be an understatement. I began to be discouraged to the point I was ready to give up my dreams of wealth. By this time Hans and I seldom spoke, but I thought he must feel the same. I wondered if I might talk him into buying out my half of the claim.

"Then, one morning after we had finished our breakfast of bread and coffee, a miracle! Hans without saying a word went down to the water's edge. I saw him bend over and seem to stare at something in the creek. Then he pulled something out, stood up, and came back to me. He held out his hand in silence.

"I looked at his palm. I too could think of no word. He held the largest nugget I had ever seen. Mind you, I don't claim it the largest ever found; only the biggest in my own experience. It lay across Hans's hand from one side to the other, and he had large hands. After a few moments he placed it in a pocket and we went back to work."

H ere Fohler and I were interrupted as an orderly brought him a noon meal. It consisted of some kind of soup with hard bread. Fohler took a little and fell silent. He seemed to be reflecting. After a minute he put it aside, wiping his chin.

. . .

"I do not know why I burden you with all this," he said. "Perhaps it were all best forgotten. And yet I feel a need to tell someone, though none of it may matter. That letter to my brother, now. I could not reveal myself to him, out of shame. I would not have my family think badly of me; ridiculous, is it not? I do not think he will learn the truth, unless he should come to California. Not that he ever would.

"As for Hans, I found myself thinking of his nugget and how to claim it. I further explored the creek in the spot where he'd discovered it, but found nothing save a few flakes. Of course I had no idea how much his nugget might be worth, but I was sure it would be enough to make our expedition almost profitable. I offered to buy it from him for my share of the gold dust, but he would have none of it. Even when I proposed to sign over my half of the claim, he said no.

"I found myself obsessed. The more Hans refused, the more I was determined to take it. The man himself did not look well, and his cough persisted. I began to hope he might fall ill enough for me to overpower him, or even to die. But I had no such luck.

"We went on like that for several weeks. There were days at a time when the subject of the nugget was never mentioned, though it never left my thoughts. Inevitably, I would bring it up again. I knew that Hans had taken to wearing the object on a cord about his neck, so I had no chance of making off with it when he slept. I must say Hans never showed impatience or lost his temper when I brought up the subject. He would simply listen to my proposals and quietly decline them. I tried to argue that since we were partners, half the value of his nugget should be mine. He shook his head and said it was not gold dust, not obtained by panning or sluicing. He had found it, and it belonged to him. He was the most stubborn man I ever met.

"Finally, there came a day when I could stand it no longer. We had both been drinking whiskey, I more than him. For several days we had found almost no color in our sluice box. Our precious store of gold dust was beginning to shrink. It came to me suddenly that I could remain on the river not a day longer. My clothing was tattered and filthy and I had not eaten a decent meal in weeks. Worst of all, there was no one to speak to besides Hans, and he conversed less and less. I had not seen a woman, honorable or otherwise, in two months. We were entirely alone at our claim; our nearest neighbors had all drifted off to greener fields. I knew if I were to remain a day longer, I would surely go mad.

"All at once, it was as if a demon had seized me. I got up from where I had been sitting near our fire and told Hans that he must give me his nugget at once. He said nothing. He merely glanced at me without interest. He took another pull at our whiskey jug and briefly shook his head.

"What I did next I did without thinking. I surely had not planned it. I was in the habit of bearing a derringer in my coat pocket. It was the kind with two barrels. The truth is, I had even forgotten that I carried it. Without a thought, I withdrew the pistol and shot him in the head. It was the first time in my life I had ever fired a pistol.

"The loud bang startled me almost back to sanity. I stared at Hans, as speechless as he was. He turned to look up to me, blood streaming down his face. He started to say something and stopped, perhaps because he could think of nothing. It appeared to me that my shot must have only grazed his skull, unless his head was hard as iron. Quickly, before he could rise, I cocked the pistol and fired my second shot into his chest.

"Even that did not kill the man. He clutched himself and fell sideways, emitting a deep groan. For a full minute I watched him lie on the ground, writhing and moaning. He said nothing, but his eyes pleaded with me. Finally I realized I must put him out of his misery. Horrified by my own act, I picked up a nearby hammer and crushed his skull."

F ohler stopped talking. For several minutes he lay in bed, staring at the ceiling as if watching the scene replay in the theater of his mind. I poured him another glass of water, which he drank slowly. Then he resumed.

.   .   .

"You can guess the rest, I suppose. I took the nugget from Hans's neck. I spent two or three hours digging a shallow grave in which to bury him. The next day I gathered our gold dust and left that place, abandoning both the claim and our equipment.

"I have not mentioned that Hans had a wife and son awaiting him in Germany. He had provided me with their address in case something should happen to him, as I had given him the address of my brother. When I got back to Sacramento, I wrote them a long letter expressing my sympathies for Hans's death from consumption. I told them what a fine man and close friend he had been to me. I promised also to send them Hans's share of our gold, once I had sold off our dust. I actually meant to do so at the time.

"But I found myself unable to part with the nugget. It had some kind of unnatural hold over me. It was as if I had traded my soul for it, and was unable to let it go. At night I would take it from my pocket and study it sometimes for hours at a time. Surely, it must be worth thousands, but I could not bring myself to sell it. The few sacks of gold dust in my possession were enough to live on for awhile, but hardly in luxury. And then I discovered that not only had I run off with Hans's nugget, I had brought along his cough. Soon I found myself acutely ill and ended up in this hospital.

"And so, Mr. Courtenay, I must beg of you one last favor. Please take the nugget. Please unburden my soul of it." He reached under his pillow, withdrew a small leather sack, and handed it to me.

"The nugget is yours, sir. I beg of you to take it and do what you will. Sell it, give it to a charity, or throw it away. I care not. It has ruined my life, and I want my freedom from it."

I opened the sack enough to peer inside. Surely it was the largest nugget I had personally seen. I had heard of larger ones, but this was indeed a champion among gold nuggets.

"I will keep it safe for you," I told him. "You may have it back when you are better. Or if you prefer, I will sell it for you."

He shook his head. "Have you heard nothing, sir? That nugget is cursed. I want nothing more to do with it. If I should come out of this place alive, please do not tell me what you did with it. And now, sir, I am feeling tired and poorly. Please leave me in peace. Please go."

And so I did, after a few parting words of farewell. I went home to enjoy Lisbeth's fine supper. A few days later I returned to the hospital to see how Mr. Fohler faired. I learned he had died only the day before. I took it on myself to purchase him a modest burial. And that was the end of Mr. Edwin Fohler's strange tale.

Oh, the nugget? You want to know what I did with it, and how much it was worth? A natural question. Drop in sometime and I will show it to you. I keep it on display on our mantel piece. It is a curiosity. Lisbeth accuses me of collecting too many knick knacks, but there it is.

About a week after Herr Fohler's burial, I took the nugget to an assayist for appraisal. He merely laughed, shook his head, and handed it back. There was no need to test it. Herr Fohler's nugget is iron pyrite—what they call fool's gold.

The End

FINDING JOAQUIN

9

SAN FRANCISCO, 1853

*A*uthor's note: Joaquin Murietta was a real person. This is not to say we know who he really was. After all these years he remains a mystery. That's what this story is about: the mystery, not the real man. When I finished writing this tale I realized it is not yet complete, the mystery not fully spun out. Therefore, at the time of this publication I am currently engaged in composing a full length novel based on the same theme. Please remain tuned.

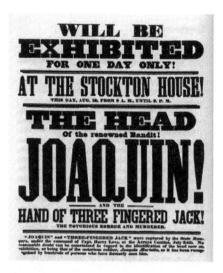

Ira Beard was a troubled man. I could see this the first time I met him. The occasion was during one of my visits to City Hall on some sort of legal business. I had just left the courtroom, and nearly bumped into him as he was strolling the corridor with Sheriff Hays. I apologized and the Sheriff, who knows me well, used the occasion to introduce us.

"Mr. Courtenay," he said. "I'm pleased to have you meet Mr. Beard." Turning to the other man, "Mr. Hyram Courtenay here is one of our oldest and most prominent citizens of this town. Been here longer than the Indians."

Mr. Beard shook my hand. I said, "The Sheriff exaggerates slightly. Lisbeth and I have been here since 1847, before it was a city, or much of a town. I'm happy to meet you, sir."

"Ira Beard," he said. "I have only been here a few days myself. I came out from New York because I'd had enough of the east and all its crowds."

The Sheriff smiled. I noticed that Beard had yet to do so. He gave me the immediate impression of a most serious gentleman. Sheriff

Hays said, "Mr. Beard is a lawman. Here he's only just arrived, and he's already chosen to take on a dangerous mission."

Hays himself was a former Texas Ranger, in fact one of the first. He would take pride in lawmen with dangerous missions. I looked to Mr. Beard, but asked no questions. He himself glanced quickly at Hays and myself, then said, "Well. There's no secret about it. I intend to go after this dangerous bandit of yours. Joaquin Murietta by name. But not for free, of course."

Hays explained, "There has been a reward offered. One thousand dollars for Murietta, dead or alive. Or for any other member of his gang. It's believed to be five in number."

Mr. Beard nodded. "If I catch all of them that would be a small fortune."

"Surely you won't go after them alone!"

He shrugged. "I have decided to take up the occupation of bounty hunting. Perhaps I may take on a deputy, or perhaps not. It should be more challenging than the New York Police."

"Indeed." With that, we exchanged our cards and parted company. It struck me odd that Mr. Beard was clean shaven despite his name. He had not smiled once. An odd gentleman, I decided. And beset by some trouble I had yet to understand.

I gave him no more thought, until about a week later when I again encountered the Sheriff at City Hall. "You'll recall that fellow Beard," he said. "The bounty hunter." I indeed remembered him.

"He's gone off," Sheriff Hays told me. "Just yesterday in fact. I tried to impress on the fellow that he had no knowledge of these California hills, or the people in them. It's not like the east. But he's a smart enough fellow, at least he listened. He hired himself two guides, one a miner and the other a Chilean fellow who can talk to the Mexicans. At least they can keep him from getting lost."

"Where is he going, exactly?" I asked.

"Well, he's after that Murietta bandit, so of course he would head for the southern mines. I think Columbia to start with, or maybe

Mariposa. I'm not sure if he knows himself. I only hope his two guides don't decide to rob him."

The year before, I had been to that area of the state myself for about two weeks, on business. I thought about Beard for a moment, trying to picture him in that setting. "There's more than Mexicans down there," I said. There's Chinese, Indians, Blacks, Irishmen and Sandwich Islanders, all trying to dig gold out of the ground. The easy placer mines have all dried up. I hope Beard knows what he's getting into."

Hays shrugged and grinned. "If he doesn't yet, he soon will."

The newspapers were filled with fresh news of the depredations of Joaquin and his gang. I read most of the stories, and soon began to doubt if all of them could be true. If they were, the Murietta-gang must have some fast horses. They seemed to be murdering all over the state, usually white English speakers. Some of the phrases I noted more than once in headlines were *terrified, citizens in fear, sleepless nights, horrible crimes, new massacres*. If this kept up, I began to wonder if there would be anyone left in California by the end of the year. Then again, Murietta's gang was responsible for the upsurge in newspaper sales.

The next time I encountered Mr. Beard he was in our hospital. This was six or seven weeks after our first meeting. I happened to see Sheriff Hays in the street. We both stopped to pass the time of day. He said, "Say. You recall that Beard fellow who said he was going after Joaquin?"

I allowed as I did. Hays said, "He's come into the hospital. I hear he was shot, but I don't know details. One of my men told me. They think he'll pull through, but I suppose he's laid up for awhile."

"I'll go and see him," I said. "I guess he probably don't have too many friends in the city."

And so I did. I found him on the second floor in his own room, sitting up in bed and reading a dime novel. At first I didn't recognize him because, unlike his previous appearance, he now sported a healthy but unruly beard and long hair. His left leg was swathed in bandages.

"Ah, Mr. Courtenay! So kind of you to visit. Boring place, this, lying around all day and trying to read. They tell me I get to keep the leg. If gangrene hasn't set in by now it won't, but it will be another week at least before I get up."

I asked if there might be anything I could bring him, food perhaps? He said he only wished for some better reading material, and perhaps a drink.

"You must have had a rough time of it," I said, being curious about his adventures.

"You could say that. I'm learning, though. I'm finding out that your western bandits are not like our eastern robbers and thugs. In New York they hide in the sewers or old buildings. Here they don't even try to hide. They can come after lawmen in force if they think they have a chance. Back east they arm themselves with knives or clubs or pistols. Here they use rifles and shotguns, sometimes swords. Dangerous work, you might say."

At his request I left Mr. Beard for a few minutes, to go across the street and purchase for him a pint flask of whiskey. When I gave it to him he offered me a drink, which I declined. He himself took a swallow and tucked the bottle under his pillow.

"We ran into a small gang of bandits," he said, after wiping his mouth. "Five or six, I think. I suppose they were Mexican, but I couldn't swear to it. Mexicans rob the whites, whites rob Mexicans and sometimes each other. Anyhow we got into a shoot out the moment we were in range. My Chilean friend was killed. I got shot myself, as you can see. My other deputy was unhurt. I believe we killed or at least wounded two or three of our bandits. When it was over with my deputy got me back to camp, but he soon left my company. No idea where he went or what his plans might be."

"Well," I said. "I guess you did your best. Will you be returning to New York now?"

He gaped at me as if I had something foolish. "Not on your tintype! Soon as this leg heals up a bit, I'm going back after Joaquin!"

The newspapers meanwhile never did let up. It would seem there were new outrages every day, all over California. Posses were formed. Most of these were not heard of again, having wandered about the woods for a few weeks and then given up. Then a new reward was offered, this time for "the Six Joaquins." I found the story so remarkable I brought a copy of the notice to Mr. Beard's attention. By now he was recuperating in a hotel room, walking with aid of a cane.

He looked over the notice, then read it through a second time. He smiled once, then shook his head as if in despair.

"The Six Joaquins. Six Mexican bandits, all with first name Joaquin, but different surnames and not related. All presumably traveling in the same gang. Incredible what some folks will make up."

"So you think the story is bogus?"

He tossed aside the paper. "Who knows what's bogus here and what not? I'm beginning to think half of all Californians are out of their minds. In San Francisco it's more like three quarters."

I asked him if he had changed his plans. He shook his head again, this time quickly. "No sir. By this time next week I believe I shall be able to ride a horse. I am still determined to go after Joaquin Murietta as long as I'm able. This time I think I shall be better prepared. A Mexican lady has been teaching me some Spanish. I think being able to speak to the natives will help me greatly."

I shook Mr. Beard's hand, wished him luck, and asked him to tell me his adventures when next he should return to our city. "Only if you promise to write them down," he said. "I hope someday to become famous."

I thought of the dime novels I had seen him read, and promised.

I did see Ira Beard another time before his departure. He stopped by my warehouse on his way out of town. He shook my hand and said, "I wanted to thank you once again for your kindness, sir. For coming to see me in my illness. And also for that pint of whiskey, for which I never did pay you."

I laughed and made to brush aside his payment, but he dropped a gold coin on my desk, several times what the bottle was worth.

"So you are still determined to go after Joaquin?"

He nodded. "You may call it a quest. Although it may turn into a duel against windmills."

"How so? Are you losing your enthusiasm?"

Once again his face changed to that vaguely troubled expression I had noted on him before. "Not exactly," he said. "But I begin to wonder at the nature of the enemy." He shoved both hands in pockets and turned as if to leave, then turned back again.

"I mentioned to you I am being tutored in Spanish. My mentor is a lady named Graciela Ortega. She is married to a restaurant owner and often works there. She also knows a great many of our local Mexicans. She has been telling me what she hears of Joaquin Murietta. The Mexicans don't think he's a bandit. In fact they see him as something of a hero. According to the story he set out to seek revenge on those who stole his land, murdered his wife, and took all he had. It seems the Murietta family is an old Spanish family from the state of Sonora. He killed those who had injured him, and then set out to right other wrongs, somewhat like a Mexican Robin Hood." Mr. Beard shrugged. "A different viewpoint, I suppose. One man's bandit is another's hero. Ah, well. I shall attempt to put a stop to his career, for better or for worse. *Hasta luego, señor.*" And with that he was off.

The next day I heard other news, this time from Sheriff Hays. I was on my way to the office of the County Clerk when he spotted me in a hallway. He shook a newspaper at me.

"Have you seen this?"

"Seen what? I have not read the papers yet."

Hays held his finger on a certain column. "They have formed a new gang to go after Murietta. They're calling them the California Rangers. Pah. They wouldn't know a ranger if they got shot by one."

I looked over the article. Well, good luck to them, I say."

"I only hope they know how to shoot," Hays said, and spat his wad into a nearby spitoon.

Now, I must tell you that by this time in our local history San Francisco was becoming a law abiding town. We'd had our problems with criminal gangs like the Sidney Ducks, but we were getting those under control. There was the usual amount of corruption and incompetence, but at least the Police Chief and Sheriff were honest. It was getting so a fellow could walk the streets without fear of being robbed or murdered. When we did have crime the papers made the most of it and that's what people remember. But most days were quiet almost to the point of boredom. I suppose that's why folks bought newspapers.

I got to thinking about my friend Ira and decided to visit his language teacher, Señora Ortega. I knew the restaurant owned by her husband; he was a German named Muller. Spanish ladies, of course, do not change their names when they marry. The establishment served fine lager beer and excellent pastries. I had no difficulty in speaking to Sra. Ortega; I already knew her from having dined there. I asked her to tell me what she had heard of Joaquin. She shrugged.

"I have a cousin, a *sobrino*, who has met him often, down at the mines. My cousin says Señor Murietta is a fine gentleman. He dresses elegantly and is most polite. It is true he sometimes robs, but he tries not to cause harm, especially not to ladies. He gives much of the money to our poor Mexican families. I know not what else to tell you, Señor."

"Do you think Mr. Beard has a chance of catching him?"

She smiled. For a moment I had a feeling she might burst into laughter. "What I fear is that Joaquin will catch Señor Beard."

Two weeks later Beard showed up again at my warehouse. He looked terrible. His clothing was torn in several places and dirty; he had not shaved in days, his face was drawn and badly sunburned. I had the impression he might be coming off a drunk. I gave him a cup of coffee.

"You are back sooner than I expected," I told him. "I thought you might be gone for months."

He sat down heavily on an upended keg. "You haven't heard, then."

"Heard what? I did glance over the *Morning Call*. Has something happened?"

"I may have arrived before the news. It seems they got him."

"Got who? You don't mean Joaquin?"

He said, "I'm thinking of returning to the east. Not New York, though. Perhaps some small town in Connecticut or Vermont which is in need of a peace officer. I spent a week or so trudging through the woods. Someone stole my pack mule. Other than that, I didn't find any bandits this time. Then I heard about the gun battle."

"Ah. What battle was that?"

"I don't recall the name of the place, if I ever heard it. They found Joaquin's camp site. There was some sort of battle, several Mexicans killed. The California Rangers are returning to San Francisco with proof of Joaquin Murietta's death. Also some fellow they call Three Finger Jack. I think they made up that name. I'm told the Mexicans called him Tres Dedos, but no one ever thought him important."

"Well," I said, "that's sensational news. I wonder what the papers will find to go on about now."

He shrugged. "As to that, I don't care. I dropped by to invite you to come with me and see."

"See what?"

"The proof. In two or three days the boys will be here with proof of Joaquin's death. It's going to be on display at the court house. I'm not sure what it is, but there's bound to be a crowd."

"Well," I said, lighting my pipe. "I surely would not wish to miss that."

· · ·

T hen the big day arrived. Ira appeared at my front gate as I was about to leave for my work, just after dawn. He leaned against the fence post, staring into space. He didn't look in a hurry, but when he saw me he just said, "Are you ready, Mr. Courtenay?"

"Ready for what?"

He said, "Well, I suppose you have not seen the posters then. They just went up last night, but they're all over town. The proof has arrived. Come on, I have a hack waiting across the road."

We climbed in and the buggy started moving. "What sort of proof is it, then?"

Beard's face held an expression I can only describe as disgusted. "Wait and see. The Sheriff alerted me last night as soon as he saw the posters. He's made arrangements for myself and a few others to view the items before the main crowd is admitted. Officially the doors don't open until noon. The admission is one dollar."

I shook my head. "That's a day's wages for a lot of folks. This must be an impressive exhibit."

At that he gave a short laugh. "I shouldn't think they will be lacking in customers."

We arrived in due course at the little museum, a little after seven. Already a crowd was gathering outside. Beard said, "If this mob gets much bigger they'll have to open the doors before noon."

Then I noted the poster on a wall near the front door. For a moment I felt a sense of shock. Then again, my mind told me I should have lived here long enough not to be shocked at much. The poster advertised *The head of Joaquin Murietta and the hand of Three Finger Jack.*

I said, "I'm not sure I want to see this."

Beard grinned. "On the other hand, I've dragged you this far. After all, this is a moment in history."

"I suppose it is at that."

A police constable checked our names and let us in through the front door. We found a small crowd gathered around a table in the middle of the main room. I noticed Sheriff Hays standing off to one side. We made our way closer, and Beard elbowed his way up to the exhibit, with me behind him. On the table I could see two large glass jars. In one was a decapitated head, in the other a human hand. The hand missed a couple of fingers. The head was immersed in what smelled like alcohol and sported a short beard that seemed to float in the liquid. The eyes were half closed, and I could not make out their color. The head's skin was a greyish caste, and I wasn't sure of the original tone.

"Ghastly," I muttered. I didn't know if anyone heard me.

All this time some fellow I had not seen before stood behind the table, recounting in loud tones his adventures of finding Joaquin and the ensuing gun battle. I only half listened, figuring the story was no doubt half lies. I looked at Beard and raised an eyebrow. He shrugged. I was about to turn away when another man approached the one who was talking. I heard him say in a low voice, "*She's here.*" The speaker stopped talking and gestured at his audience to move back.

"Gentlemen! Please step back a few paces and make room for an important witness. Now, there have been some skeptical questions from those who doubt that this might not be the actual Joaquin Murietta, of statewide fame! I have arranged to have Joaquin's sister brought here to identify this face. Of course we already have several signed affidavits from other witnesses, which you may view at your leisure. Joaquin's actual sister will put the final stamp on this business. Please make way for Señorita Murietta!"

A young woman moved from somewhere in back to near the table. She was dressed entirely in black, wearing a veil so that I could not make out her features. She was escorted by a large man in formal clothing and wearing a badge, who I took to be some sort of lawman. The lady moved slowly to the table without speaking. Standing straight, she stopped in front of the two jars and seemed to be staring at the disembodied head. I half expected her to fall over in a faint. Instead, after remaining still for about a minute, she abruptly turned and walked away, her guard following. She had not made a sound.

The man who had been speaking coughed, cleared his throat, and made an odd little bow. "No doubt the señorita is overcome with emotion. We shall collect her signed statement when she has composed herself. Now, getting back to my narrative of our gun battle ..."

Beard gave me a nudge. "Let's leave."

I did not argue.

I returned to my work at the warehouse. Beard and I were both silent until we parted. That evening I told my wife Lisbeth something of what I had seen, but she could tell I was not eager to discuss the matter. Truth is, I would have preferred to forget. About a week later I received a note from Mr. Beard:

S ir,
   I shall be departing San Francisco in a few days, with passage booked on the Panama steamer. I have enjoyed your company while here, and am still grateful for the whiskey. Perhaps you might join me for lunch at my hotel?

A nd so I did see Mr. Beard one last time. I recall the weather cold and drizzly that day, casting a somber mood. I was glad for hot soup rather than my usual lunch of cold meat and cheese.

Mr. Beard said, "She would not sign."

"Who? Sign what?

He chewed thoughtfully for a moment. "I will miss your California oysters and bay shrimp. Murietta's sister. She would not sign the affidavit. She says that was not her brother."

I put down my spoon to stare at him. "Then who was it, for God's sake?"

He shrugged. "Who knows? Some bandit, I suppose. Or maybe just an innocent miner. Do you know they will be taking that head and hand on tour all over California? Even to the mining camps. Perhaps someone will actually recognize him. In any event, there are dozens who will swear it's Joaquin. Perhaps the sister lied, for reasons of her own. I hear the legislature has voted to award the Rangers an extra five thousand dollars for apprehending the man."

I closed my eyes a moment, thinking. "Then, if it's not Joaquin, that means the real Joaquin is still on the loose. He will yet be committing further depredations and atrocities."

At that Beard gave a little smile. "Is that what it means? Or does it only mean he's sold enough newspapers, and kept people excited as long as he could. Perhaps Joaquin has used up his usefulness. Perhaps Joaquin never actually existed. Perhaps Joaquin was a bogey man."

He paused a moment. "The Spanish took the land from the Indians. Then we took it from them. Perhaps we are afraid someone will take the land from us, or Mexico may take it back. Joaquin is a fear that we can name. To the Mexicans Joaquin is revenge. Either way, he will make a grand story. What is your opinion?"

I ate my soup in silence. Finally I said, "I hope, sir, that you will write to me from the east. By the time I answer I may have formed an opinion."

"Indeed I shall." He stared out the window at our soft rain. "I think California is beyond my understanding. Perhaps in a hundred years it will be more like the United States. Perhaps by that time you will have truly found your Joaquin."

And with that we parted. It rained all week, and there was peace.

MRS. HINKLE'S FINISHING SCHOOL FOR YOUNG LADIES

10

SAN FRANCISCO, 1857

Welcome to San Francisco. I thought as long as we're both waiting for the boat to Sacramento, we might as well get acquainted. Since there's no one here to introduce us properly, we need not stand on ceremony, as they might back in Boston or New York. My name is Lisbeth Courtenay. My husband is Hyram, and he's a warehouseman here. No, we're not native to California, but we have been here since forty-seven, before the Rush, so I guess we might as well be born here. You say you're meeting your husband in Sacramento? Been mining gold, has he? I hope he's had some luck.

I must say there's a good deal of luck going around these days, both the good kind and the bad. If you should ever get to meet Hyram, no doubt you will hear some stories of both good and evil. But please take what you might hear with a grain of salt. I don't say Hyram makes things up, but he does tend to colorize the truth at times.

Well, you're right. I do have a few stories of my own, I guess. I just don't tell them as often. Have you been in California for long? Six months, is it? Stick around awhile longer, you shall have stories of your own to relate.

My business in Sacramento? You might say it's a shopping spree.

Not for myself, though. I help to manage a finishing school for young ladies, and we are in need of supplies, including some furniture and cotton for making dresses. You see, a lot of ships prefer to dock there instead of San Francisco because of the harbor facilities. Hyram tells me we are working to fix that, with new wharfs and all.

I don't know if you have heard of our school. We do not advertise. It's called Mrs. Hinkle's Finishing School for Young Ladies. This does remind me of a tale.

There is no Mrs. Hinkle. That's just a made-up name. We wanted it to sound as respectable as possible. I must confess the original idea was my own. I talked it over with some other ladies in my church, and we agreed it was a good idea. Reverend Beaverhill took some convincing, but he came around when we got to raising funds through public subscription. We were able to purchase an old house on Dupont Street for two hundred dollars. Then it was just a matter of finding a manager and a school teacher, and we were in business.

It's not exactly a finishing school, you see. You must have noticed by now that in this city the men vastly outnumber the women here. A lot of the single women are from places like Chile, China, and Mexico. A couple of years ago we had a sudden influx of ladies and men from France. That was because Louis Napoleon was busy cleaning out his prisons, but that's another subject.

Well, you can figure out what happens in a place where we have so few women and so many lonely men. We do have a great many fallen doves. A lot of the French girls were practicing their trade back in the old country, but they can make hundreds of times here what they got back there. It's just the way of the world. Hyram tells me a lonesome miner will often give a girl a poke of gold just to sit and talk with him awhile.

Of course some of the miners are married, but that's no problem. In fact some of them are married to girls they met in a parlor house. The other wives put up with it because it keeps the men folk out of worse trouble. What I'm getting at is the reason we decided to start up the finishing school. We figured some of those ladies would just as soon find another way of life, given half a chance. Not many, but a few. As Christian ladies, we felt it was up to us to offer them a chance.

The school is located within two or three blocks of all the cribs and parlor houses, which tend to stay in their own part of town. Everybody knows about the school. We don't advertise, but word gets around. When a young lady decides she's had enough she comes to our school, and we make room for her. Usually we have only six or seven at a time. We try to educate them if they need educating, teach them manners if they don't have any, and get them placed in a respectable job, like maid or cook. We have a few prayer meetings, but we try not to lay the religion on too thick. Reverend Beaverhill is supposed to be the school president, but it's actually run by us ladies.

The story I'm reminded of is that of Mademoiselle Estee Mirabeau. She showed up one day not long after the school first opened. At the time we only had three other students. We had high hopes at the time. Some of the other ladies had dreams of closing down all the cribs and houses, but I guess I knew better than that. I would have been happy to save one or two women.

Mademoiselle means Miss in French. I've had to learn to talk a few words of that lingo because so many of our ladies are from that country. Well, Miss Mirabeau showed up early one morning on our doorstep. I should say I assumed at the moment she was a miss, but that turned out to be wrong, her being a widow, which I didn't find out till later. I answered the bell, and there she was all by herself. It took me a moment to look her over. She was wearing an old tattered dress with a few patches on it. She held a cloth sack by the neck, and I guessed it probably had her few possessions. I would have taken her for a common fallen lady, except there was something different about the way she was looking at me. I'd have to say it was a haughty look, chin up high and looking me straight in the eye. I noticed her hair was nicely braided, as if someone had spent some careful time doing it.

I was trying to think what to say, and if I should use English or

French, but she spoke up first. "Good morning," she says. "I am the Marquise Estee Mirabeau. I am here to request sanctuary."

Well, you could have knocked me over. We have a lot of folks around here who claim to be dukes or marquies or such, but they're usually card sharps or politicians. But this lady standing before me gave me such an odd feeling, like maybe she really was what she claimed. It must have been her way of speaking, with a little accent, but her proper English I guess was better than my own. Of course I had to invite her in.

I introduced her to our other ladies and showed her the room she would share with another. By good fortune we had another French lady at the time, who I knew only as Marie. The two babbled a few minutes in their own tongue, and Marie said she would be delighted to share a room. She gave a little curtsey and went off to make a bed ready. Meanwhile I tried to explain to our new student what we would try to do for her. I got as far as the part about teaching her to read. A lot of our other students never got to the first grade, if that. Miss Mirabeau interrupted me. Up till then, she hadn't said a word since I let her in, except in French to Marie.

She waved a hand and said, "You need not mind my education, Madam. I assure you I am literate in French, English, German and some Spanish. May I inquire about meals?"

At that I felt embarrassed, since it hadn't even occurred to me Miss Mirabeau might be hungry. In fact, taking another look at her face I could see her cheeks were sunken as if she'd gone without a few suppers. "Why, of course," I told her. "Supper will be in about an hour. I'm afraid the fare is simple, but there's lots of it, much as you want. The ladies all take turns in the kitchen, but we'll give you a day or two to rest up before you're asked to pitch in."

She raised no objection and just said she would like to lie down a bit before supper. I brought her back to her room to make sure she had enough bedding and closet space. I noticed the little bag she'd brought in and asked her if that was all her clothes?

"Yes, I'm afraid so. Perhaps if you could aid me in finding some cloth and sewing tools I might correct this problem. I am something of an amateur seamstress, you see. If any of the other ladies have garments in need of mending I should be happy to help."

I told her, "That would be wonderful, Marquise. None of our other ladies have much acquaintance with needles and thread. Perhaps you might instruct them."

"I should be most happy," she said, and lay down with all her clothes on. I could see she was run out, so I left her there and went home to make Hyram's dinner.

I thought no more of our marquise for some time. With all my other chores, I could usually visit the school no more than once or twice a week. Some of our ladies remained there as long as six months or a year, while others might move in and out almost before you noticed them. I do recall seeing Miss Mirabeau several times, but she seemed always to be busy sewing. She did appear much better dressed than when she had first arrived. Her face and figure were filling out as well.

Then one evening Hyram answered a knock on our door to find an odd looking little man with a briefcase. "Good evening," he said, with some kind of accent to his voice. I thought he might be Australian or South African. "Mr. Courtenay?" he said. Hyram allowed as he was that person.

"Might I have the honor of speaking to the lady of the house?" he says. "I am Martin Deville, of the firm of Wharwood and Meade, London solicitors."

Hyram didn't quite know what to make of that, but he decided to find out what the fellow had to say, so he let him in. He was a short stubby fellow with a red nose and round belly. Hyram introduced us and asked if he would like to sit down or have a drink.

"No thank you," he says. "I won't need but a moment of your time. I am given to understand that Mrs. Courtenay is manager of Mrs. Hinkle's Finishing School, am I correct?"

"One of the managers," I said. "We more or less take turns. What may I do for you, sir?"

"It's a matter of a lawsuit," he says. "I was told that men are not allowed to enter your school unless accompanied by the manager. It so happens I have learned that a certain Marquise Estee Mirabeau resides there at present. I should like very much to interview this lady."

"She's really a marquise, then? Well, sir, what's this about, then?"

Mr. Deville dug into his case and pulled out a piece of paper. He sort of waved it like a fan. "The marquise is named in a civil suit in France. She owns an estate in Provence, which is claimed by the Bank of London in payment of debts. Debts incurred by the marquise's husband, now deceased. I'm afraid it's a complicated case, given the current unrest on the continent and other factors."

I didn't know what to say, so I looked to Hyram. He gave a shrug. "I suppose it would do no harm to let you speak to her, if she's willing." He looked at me. "I'll go along, if you like."

"All right," I said. Then I asked Mr. Deville, "Has Miss Mirabeau done anything wrong? Is she accused of any crimes?"

"No, no." Deville shook his head. "However, if she were still in Europe she might be at risk of debtor's prison."

Well, the interview took place two days later. Mrs. Mulligan was running the school that day. Miss Mirabeau had to be pulled out of a cooking class she was teaching. Mrs. Mulligan took me aside for a moment.

"Our new lady is a wonder," she whispered. "She's been giving some of our French girls English lessons. She is also making dresses and gowns, so they might look their best. I will have her show you some."

Of course I was pleased to hear this, but I didn't want to miss anything Mr. Deville had to say, so I hurried in to the room where he was waiting. Hyram closed the door so we should have some privacy. The marquise entered the room as if she owned the place and took a comfortable chair, then she just waited.

Mr. Deville offered her a low bow. "Madam Marquise," he began. "It is an honor. I have traveled from England and France, around the Horn to see you. I am sure you must have some inkling of why I am here."

At that Miss Mirabeau gave a little laugh. "Monsieur," she said. "I shall address you in English, as you have me, although I am sure you are more comfortable in French. Yes, monsieur, I know exactly why you are here. You need not address me as Marquise. The title is hereditary, but without meaning since all such titles were abolished by the revolution. I myself am a republican, which is one reason Louis despises me and has gone to such expense to send you here. Do not deny your expedition is funded by the government of France."

Mr. Deville's face turned a little red, and he loosened his collar. "Madam," he said, "I represent an international corporation which has an interest in securing your estate as payment of debt. As to the government—"

Miss Mirabeau turned toward Hyram and me and interrupted before he could finish. "The fact is," she said, "my late husband Francois was snookered into running up some heavy debts in order to pay taxes on the estate. The taxes were imposed by Louis Napoleon's cronies in an effort to gain legal control of our property. The tax was paid, so now they are attempting to collect the debt. However, the first payment does not fall due until next year. I heard that Louis planned to have me arrested as a political dissident."

Miss Mirabeau glanced at Deville and gave him a broad smile, then turned and gave me a wink. "I therefore chose to visit California. I was forced to bribe my way aboard an emigrant ship which was being used to deport some of the fallen ladies from the Paris prison. I must say my fellow passengers were more *amaiblee* than many I left behind, especially in the government."

Hyram and I could not help but stare at each other. Neither of us had ever heard such a strange story, and we had both heard many others. Miss Mirabeau then turned to regard Deville. "I believe that about summarizes my position, sir. You may now speak your piece."

Deville had meanwhile taken some papers from his case, which he held out toward Miss Mirabeau. She ignored them.

He said, "Madam, I shall not bore our guests with a rebuttal. The situation now is quite simple. If you will but sign this deed of transfer, your debts will be canceled. You will be free of all encumbrances. If not, further legal proceedings may go ahead. Although it is true your first payment is not yet due, it may require months to transfer funds, and we therefore are demanding a commitment now. Our Mr. Courtenay may witness your signature."

She still would not so much as glance at the papers. "And what legal proceedings do you refer to, sir?"

At this he put down the papers on a low table. He gave a shrug. "Madam, there are warrants for your arrest both in England and France. The charges are fraud, default of legal debt, and sedition. Extradition proceedings may begin."

"I see." She gave Mr. Deville a broad smile. "In that case, sir, I believe our business is at an end. May you have a fine day."

Deville took the hint and turned toward the door, after giving us a bow. "I leave the document for your perusal, Madam. You may wish to have an attorney look it over. If you should change your mind and decide to sign, the paper may be delivered to the French Consul within ten days. After that, further actions will result." Then he turned and left the room. I heard Mrs. Mulligan showing him out.

Madam Mirabeau smiled at us both. "The estate is our ancestral property, you see. I'm afraid it's in a state of great neglect at present. I have never actually lived there except for occasional visits. My husband the Marquis was never able to afford to keep up the place. Probably by now the roof of the main house has fallen in. But Louis thinks it would add to his prestige to claim it as a summer place. He sees this as a chance at another public blow at the aristocracy – namely, myself."

She paused a moment and looked at our faces, perhaps trying to see if we understood. I wasn't sure I did. Then she said, "You see, Louis Napoleon would like to be an aristocrat himself. He doesn't understand that France is now a republic."

· · ·

Before Hyram and I left the school Mrs. Mulligan insisted on showing us an upstairs closet. Madam Mirabeau followed along behind. Mrs. Mulligan paused before the closet door before opening it.

"You must see what Lady Mirabeau has been up to!" This was the first time I'd heard anyone refer to Estee Mirabeau as Lady. I didn't think it was a correct title, but I didn't say anything, being unsure myself. Later on, everyone else began calling her Lady Mirabeau and she never tried to correct them.

"She has remarkable talent, as you shall see!" Mrs. Mulligan opened the closet, to display a collection of the most beautiful gowns and dresses I had ever seen. Mrs. Mulligan began pulling them out one at a time, then re-hanging them on their pegs. Hyram had a blank look. I guess he'd never seen the like either, but I don't think he knew what to make of them. In fact he had never before been inside our Finishing School, and I suppose he wasn't feeling quite right about being there.

"The Lady has been making these for our ladies here," Mrs. Mulligan was saying. "In case they should wish to attend a ball or the concert. In fact, three of our girls was at the theater last week and made quite a splash! Madame Belle Cora was there and took notice. She said she wishes to commission some dresses for her own girls."

Belle Cora, you understand, operates one of our best parlor houses. She's in the habit of parading her girls on Sunday in the Plaza, riding in a brougham and dressed in their best finery.

Madam Mirabeau spoke up. "It has always been a hobby of mine. I like to design ladies' clothing. Mine are all in the latest Parisian styles. At first I was at a loss to find suitable cloth, but I soon discovered that some of your Chinese merchants have the finest silks and other materials." Turning to me she said, "I should be happy to make a gown for you, Madam, free of charge. You would be most elegant."

I laughed. "Elegant is not something I need, Mrs. Mirabeau. Broadcloth will do me just fine. We had best be going, Hyram. Your warehouse awaits."

I think Hyram was relieved to get out of there.

Well, it turned out that indeed Belle Cora commissioned some dresses and gowns. I only heard about that because it got mentioned on the social page of one of our newspapers, the *Alta* I think it was. Everyone at the Plaza noticed the new styles of Madam Cora's ladies and herself. Somehow the reporter wheedled out the information about who had designed those gowns. I think he must have got it from one of Belle Cora's girls, because I'm sure she herself never would have revealed it. So suddenly everybody in town was aware that the new styles were the work of "Lady Mirabeau."

Now it so happened I had other things to worry about, so I didn't get back to the school for several weeks. The next time I visited I found Mrs. Costello in charge. Of course I asked after Madam Mirabeau. Mrs. Costello just shrugged.

"She left about a week ago. Such goings on! She said she had a couple big commissions for new gowns and was moving to a hotel. I have her address somewhere if you want it. Before she left she handed me two hundred dollars silver, said it was for her room and board. I told her that was too much but she insisted. Naturally I turned it over to Reverend Beaverhill."

A few days after that, being in the neighborhood I went to visit the lady in her new digs. Sure enough, she had a suite at the Palace. Not just one room, but three. When I knocked on the door a girl answered. I knew her as one of our previous students at the school. Of course she recognized me and let me in. I found Madam Mirabeau seated at a desk covered with papers of various sizes. She'd been cutting up some of them with scissors. When she saw me she jumped up and gave me a hug.

"Such a delight!" she said. "If only you had let me know you were to come, I might have had refreshments. But I am happy to see you! Do you like my little studio?"

Looking around, the place resembled more a factory than a studio. Three girls I didn't know were busy sewing, and there were various kinds of material all over the place, including rolls of silk in several colors.

"More commissions than I can handle!" She waved a hand at the girls. They looked up and grinned. "Mrs. Nesbitt up on Nob Hill noticed Belle Cora's ladies with their new gowns. She was jealous and came in person to see me. She wore a creation of mine to a neighbor's ball, and before I could *think* several of your other San Francisco socialites desired my styles. It seems this city is hungry for the French appearance."

"It is indeed a lovely style. I might order a gown myself, but I expect Hyram would be scandalized."

"Rubbish!" She waved away the notion. "Men know nothing, they have to be told what is good! Please allow me to take your measure."

Before I could stop her, she produced a tape and began measuring me. "You should have a new corset," she said. "This one does not justice to your bosoms."

"Speaking of justice," I said, "how goes our legal problems?"

She gave another dismissive wave. "I do not give a fig. I spoke to an attorney, though. He says there would be great difficulties with extradition, it is not a worry. With all the money I have made, I could pay off my debts, but let them have the estate if they must. I only refuse out of spite. Perhaps Louis Napoleon will have a conniption fit!"

Suddenly I heard a mechanical whirring sound from the back of the room. Seeing my interest, Madam Mirabeau led me over. A girl was seated before a small table with some kind of machine on it. She was busy spinning a large wheel, while a skein of blue cloth moved beneath it. The girl, intent on her work, did not so much as glance up.

"It's a sewing machine," Madam Mirabeau explained. "Very hard to come by. This one was made in France. Soon I suppose everyone will have them, but for now I have the great advantage."

"Indeed." I bent over the better to study the device, but I could not imagine how it worked, even watching. Madam Mirabeau told me it made lock stitches, so I took her word for it. I said to her, "It's all a wonderment, isn't it?"

. . .

During the next few weeks "Lady Mirabeau" took San Francisco society by storm. The upper crust here is not a large club, compared to your eastern cities, so it wasn't long before every matron and daughter in town wanted something designed by Lady Mirabeau. In fact, you could say she single handed changed our style. Others began to copy her fashions and it was not long before no lady in the city would appear in public unless she were dressed in the French style. By the way, Madam Mirabeau did make for me a beautiful gown. I wore it next time Hyram took me to the theater, but I'm not sure if he noticed. He's a man, what do you expect?

The next thing was that I heard that Madam Mirabeau had taken up with Mr. Meade, the lumber baron. Mr. Meade, of course, is quite wealthy. He also has a wife and three children, two boys and a girl. I'm sure you have lived here long enough not to be scandalized by such news. Such arrangements are not uncommon with the wealthier gentry. Often the lady of the house will choose to ignore the affair, since it may serve to relieve her of some marital obligations. At least it gets the man away a few days a month for "business trips." Then the lady can enjoy her own freedom.

Mr. Meade set Lady Mirabeau up in a large downtown store, away from that hotel. She continued to live at the Palace, but was able to expand her dressmaking business. Of course it was not long before one could find less expensive versions in some of the stores. I must say even the imitations brought a new sense of grace and beauty to our city that was not there before. From what I hear, some ladies have returned to the eastern states and are spreading these fashions every-where. It's all a wonderment.

Well, what happened next was that Mr. Deville showed up again on our doorstep. This was in the evening just as I was preparing to put supper on the table. Hyram answered a loud pounding and there he was, looking like a red faced toy soldier. "*I must speak to you at once, sir!*" he says.

"Well," Hyram says in reply, "don't see why not. Such a nice surprise. Come on in, have a seat. I can have Lisbeth set another place at the table."

Deville sort of pushed Hyram aside and entered. He stared straight at me. "Madam!" he says to me. "I must know where Madam Mirabeau has gone!"

I gave him a shrug and looked at Hyram. My husband stepped between the two of us. "Now, Mr. Deville, sir, there's no need to speak in a rude tone to my missus. Why don't you sit down, cool off a bit, and tell us what's the matter?"

Deville took a deep breath and looked at Hyram, who was quite a bit larger than himself. He said, "Sir, I am sorry if I have offended. It's just that I am quite upset. I was hoping that Mrs. Courtenay might know the whereabouts of the Marquise. The fact is, I went with a constable this afternoon to her hotel suite, in order to place her under arrest. The papers for extradition have finally come through. If she still refuses to pay her legal debt to our bank, she is to be arrested and deported to France."

"I see." Hyram turned and took a cup of coffee from the table where he had set it down when Deville knocked on our door. He sipped it and looked over the rim at our visitor. "And what happened when you went to her hotel, sir?"

Deville pounded a fist into his palm. I have heard of men doing that sometimes, but I believe this was the first time I had ever seen it done. "She was gone! Checked out a week ago, I was told! No forwarding address! We then proceeded to her storefront, the constable and myself. I found several ladies at work there. But the Marquise had scarpered. She sold her business and left the premises before vacating the hotel."

"Ah." Hyram nodded. "And I guess she left no address. So you supposed she might have told Mrs. Courtenay where she was headed. Is that the size of it?"

"Yes sir. Except that the new owner of her business claimed that the Marquise was leaving on a ship headed back to France. Given her legal position, I can not credit that story."

At this point I had to speak up. "She didn't tell me where she was going," I said. "But on several occasions when we spoke together, Lady Mirabeau expressed a desire to return to her native estate in France. She thought California lovely, but it's not France, as she put it."

Hyram said, "If she left a week ago it would have been before you got the extradition papers. She would not have known about it yet."

"I suppose that's true, sir. And yet she probably had some inkling it was about to happen. Don't ask me how. I can not believe she would return with such debt facing her. And her political position ..."

"From what I read in the papers," Hyram said, "Louis Napoleon has begun to loosen his hold on members of the opposition, letting some of them out of jail and so on."

Deville stared in the direction of our fireplace. "Yes, and relaxing the censorship laws. It's a pity, I say." Suddenly he turned red in the face and stamped his foot on the floor. "*I won't have it!* If the Marquise has escaped I shall forfeit my commission. I won't have it!"

At this I could see Hyram try to repress a smile. "Well, sir. I have your card. If we should hear anything of the Lady's whereabouts I shall certainly inform you at once."

Then Mr. Deville gave us both a black look. Without saying another word he turned and stomped out the door.

That was about the last we heard of the matter, until some eight months later when a letter arrived by way of Panama steamer. It was from Lady Mirabeau herself, and postmarked from France. I believe we still have it somewhere. I can remember most of what it says:

. . .

My dear American friends,

Greetings from la Belle France. I am so happy. I should say we are all so happy, Mr. and Mrs. Meade and the children. You see, all has been arranged. After discussing the matter, we decided to create a menage a trois as we call it here. Both the Meades are quite agreeable, and the children are such dears. We have paid off all my debts, and Louis N. has forgiven my crimes. Mr. Meade has been most generous in helping to renovate my family estate. We shall reside here during the summer, and are using the property to house a 'finishing school,' of the same type as your own in San Francisco. You all have been such an inspiration. Already we have six girls paroled from the Paris prison and learning to become ladies. We look forward to a bright future. Please share as much of this letter as you wish with your friends in California. I enclose a modest bank note as a donation to your school.

With great love, Estee.

So you see, that is my story about the Marquise Estee Mirabeau. An unusual tale, don't you think? Oh, but I see our boat is docking. We had best gather our luggage, it's time to board. What's that you say? You want to know what became of Mr. Martin Deville? He did well for a time. He decided not to return to his former position in England. Or perhaps he was fired, I'm not sure. He went into banking here in San Francisco. At the time we were desperately in need of banks, and it did not require much capital to start one. What banks we had were minting their own money with California gold. Then Mr. Deville was caught out when someone analyzed his coins and found they had a large copper content. Mr. Deville bribed his way out of jail, left town and has not been seen since.

Now let's get on board and enjoy the scenery. It's all a wonderment, *n'est pas?*

THE END

If you have enjoyed these brief tales, please visit the author's website at www.stevebartholomew.com.

You may view my other books at amzn.to/1QcsUb5

And please consider writing a review.

BONUS CHAPTER

HEREWITH AN EXCERPT FROM MY
NOVEL TUNNEL 6

GERALDINE

From the journal of Geraldine Halloran, November 3, 1866:

I resolve not to be terrified. I am told this will be a dangerous place for a woman. But Ma told me I can decide whether to scare or not, and I choose not. This train is cold despite the blanket around me; snow covers all outside. How can the engine even move through this snow? The few men aboard give me strange looks. One of them has told me there is but one other woman in camp, that being Mrs. Strobridge, the supervisor's wife. Perhaps I have made a terrible error in coming here, but I resolve to see it through, without fear.

The work train bore no conductor to carry her bag or to help her down the steps. Fortunately she had only one small bag to carry, and that with all her worldly possessions. The engine sat snuffling and clanking and complaining, as engines will.

Geraldine Halloran looked around for help. She could see a few sheds and some tents, and a great deal of snow. Parked on a siding were three passenger cars. She decided to head in that direction, but a large man on horseback cut her off. He was a really large man, wearing a voluminous fur coat that made him look bigger.

"What are you doing here?"

She *would* not show fear. She put down her bag and tilted her head back to stare up at the man. "I have every business to be here. I am hired on."

The man folded his arms and spat out a plug of tobacco, which steamed a moment in the fresh snow. "We have no need of maids or laundresses up here. This is a railroad work camp."

"Yes, sir. I know that. And I will not be needing a maid nor a laundress either. I hear you have a Chinese laundry here. I am hired on as telegraph operator."

"What?" The man unfolded his arms. "I hired a telegrapher myself, yesterday. That is, I ordered our office in Sacramento to hire one and send him up." He withdrew a rumpled telegraph form from an inner pocket. "'Telegrapher arrive tomorrow work train. Name Jerry Halloran.'"

"Yes, sir. That would be me. Geraldine Halloran, formerly of Western Pacific Telegraph Company, Sacramento branch. I can send and receive twenty words per minute."

The man muttered something under his breath. Then he climbed down from the saddle, dropping his horse's reins to the ground. The steed gave a deep cough, relieved of its burden. The man gave a quick bow. "Forgive me for my rudeness. Frankly, I would have preferred a man, but the fact is we're desperate at the moment. Our telegrapher quit without notice, saying he could abide here no longer. Since you're here, I suppose we'll have to give you a trial. I have numerous dispatches awaiting transmission. Come with me, please. My name is Charles. Charles Crocker. I own this railroad."

The Morse shack turned out to actually be a box car. It held a telegraph key, as well as a bunk and a couple of chests. A small potbelly stove that had apparently not been lit for a day or so sat in a corner; it felt as cold inside the shack as out. Geraldine gathered her wool shawl about her and sat down at a rough wood table that served as a desk. She rubbed her stiff fingers together a moment, then pulled the key to her and clicked off a quick CQ. After a moment the key clicked back in acknowledgment.

Charles Crocker hovered by her shoulder. She turned to look at him. "What do you want me to send?"

He pulled a folder from a nearby box and plopped it in front of her. "These dispatches have been waiting two days. The one on top is the most urgent. Come and see me at the supervisor's cabin when you're done." He waited a moment, watching as her fingers began tapping the key. He turned to go, then paused at the door. "I'll have someone bring some wood and start your fire." He pulled the door open, but paused a second time. "And please don't be startled should you hear an explosion. That will be blasting in the tunnel." He went out, shutting the door behind him.

Geraldine had not paused in transmitting while Crocker was speaking. She barely heard him, registering his words with a separate part of her brain. The urgent dispatch he'd given her concerned shipping more supplies at once. In fact, chemicals: nitric acid, glycerine, sulfuric acid. She had no idea what use those would be; she merely transmitted words. At one point as she paused between papers, the key clicked a brief response: the Morse code meaning "please slow down." Geraldine grinned and did her best to comply. It took her nearly an hour to get though the dispatches. When she was done with the last sheet she tapped out "GG, GOH." The last three letters were her personal signature. The GG meant "I'm going." The key responded with "R, RUM," R meaning "received," with the other operator's sign-off. Geraldine wondered who RUM was; she didn't know anyone with that sign, and there were not that many telegraphers in Sacramento. She shrugged and pushed the key away.

Her fingers were cold and getting stiff, but as she finished she realized the stove was lit and the deadly chill in the shack had lost some edge. She hadn't noticed anyone come in. Moving to the stove, she held her hands above it. She would have to find her gloves, the ones without fingertips. Next thing was to locate the supervisor's shack; back out in the snow. As she eased the door open and stepped into the cold, she was startled to find a Chinese man waiting by the door.

"Missy Jerry?" He was grinning.

"Yes. Jerry, Geraldine. Did you light my stove while I was working?"

"Yes, missy. You please follow me." He turned without another word and walked off. She shrugged and followed, trying to keep up in the several inches of new snow. Her feet were getting wet and cold. "Where are we going? What's your name?"

He answered without looking back. "Mister Stro shack. Ling."

She took a moment to process the information. Mister Stro would be Strobridge, the chief supervisor. She guessed Ling was the Chinese man's name. He took her to another, somewhat larger shack on the outskirts of camp. As she was about to enter there was a deep thud that seemed to come from underground. The snow itself seemed to jump.

Ling looked back at her, still grinning. "Boom in tunnel," he explained.

Geraldine entered the shack to find a man in workman's clothes seated behind a crude table. On the opposite side stood two other men, both heavily bearded and dressed. They turned to stare as she entered. The man at the table glanced at her, then turned back to the men. She was startled by the ferocious appearance of his face, which was not helped by a black patch over one eye. It made her think of pirates.

"That will be all, gentlemen. I must have a word with our new telegraph operator, Miss Halloran. I'm sure you will see she is treated with the utmost courtesy. I'll have you both back here in the morning." Both men nodded and went out. Strobridge stood up and gave her a little bow. "Please be seated a moment, miss. Those were two of my foremen. Permit me a moment to make some notes." He bent over a ledger and scribbled something in ink, then looked up at her. He was not smiling.

"I believe you are here under somewhat false pretenses. Or

perhaps just a misunderstanding. We were expecting a male operator."

She shrugged. "I had no wish to deceive. There was a call for a volunteer to join the Central Pacific Railroad. I was the only person in my office willing to come here."

"I see." He stared at her a moment, his eyes cold as snow. "Well, Miss Halloran. You will find the life here is hard and sometimes dangerous. The pay is better than what you may be used to, but that has not prevented turnover. We have had four operators quit in the last six months. And I'm afraid you may be a disruptive influence in our camp. Not with the Chinese workers, they're quite civilized. They don't get drunk or brawl. But they refer to our white foremen and workers as barbarians. I often suspect they are right about that."

She sat up straight in her chair. "I will do my best not to become disruptive."

He nodded, watching her. He said, "Tell me this, Miss Halloran. Why did you volunteer for the railroad? It could not have been just the extra pay."

It was a moment before she answered. She considered telling the truth, how she was weary of working in a room with five other women and five other telegraph keys with their constant chatter—the keys, not the women, who seldom had time for talk. She hated the constant supervision of the male manager, who reminded her of a third grade school master. She even rebelled against having to wear a corset at all times: obviously, one must dress proper while at the key! Instead she lied, looking him in the eye. "Well, sir, it's like this. As a child I always wanted to run off with the circus. But everyone said I wasn't good looking enough for that. Nor was I ugly enough for the freak show. Then, last year, I saw a railroad locomotive for the first time. It was splendid, with all its clanking iron and black smoke and steam. I fell in love at once. I knew then it would be my destiny to run away, not with the circus, but with the railroad."

And she gave him her brightest smile.

Made in the USA
Middletown, DE
02 February 2020